THE Pearl-shell Diver

A story of adventure from the Torres Strait

THE Pearl-shell Diver

KAY CRABBE

First published by Allen & Unwin in 2016

Allen & Unwin
83 Alexander Street
Crows Nest NSW 2065
Australia
Phone: (61 2) 8425 0100
Email: info@allenandunwin.com
Web: www.allenandunwin.com

A Cataloguing-in-Publication entry is available from the
National Library of Australia www.trove.nla.gov.au

ISBN (AUS) 978 1 76029 047 4

Teachers' notes available from www.allenandunwin.com

Consultant editor: Lyn White
Cover and text design by Debra Billson
Cover images by Tim Gerard Barker / Getty Images (Torres Strait Islander boy), The Print Collector / Alamy (1886 etching) and Teacept / Shutterstock
Additional text illustrations from State Library of Victoria and Morphart / Canstock
Set in 11/16 pt Sabon Roman by Midland Typesetters
Printed in Australia by McPherson's Printing Group

10 9 8 7 6 5 4 3 2 1

MIX
Paper from responsible sources
FSC
www.fsc.org
FSC® C001695

The paper in this book is FSC® certified. FSC® promotes environmentally responsible, socially beneficial and economically viable management of the world's forests.

More than a hundred islands lie in the Torres Strait waters between the tip of Australia's Cape York Peninsula and Papua New Guinea. Seventeen are inhabited. The people of the Torres Strait Islands are saltwater people – fishers and sea-farers. Their customs, culture and identity differ from those of Aboriginal people of mainland Australia.

This is Sario's story . . .

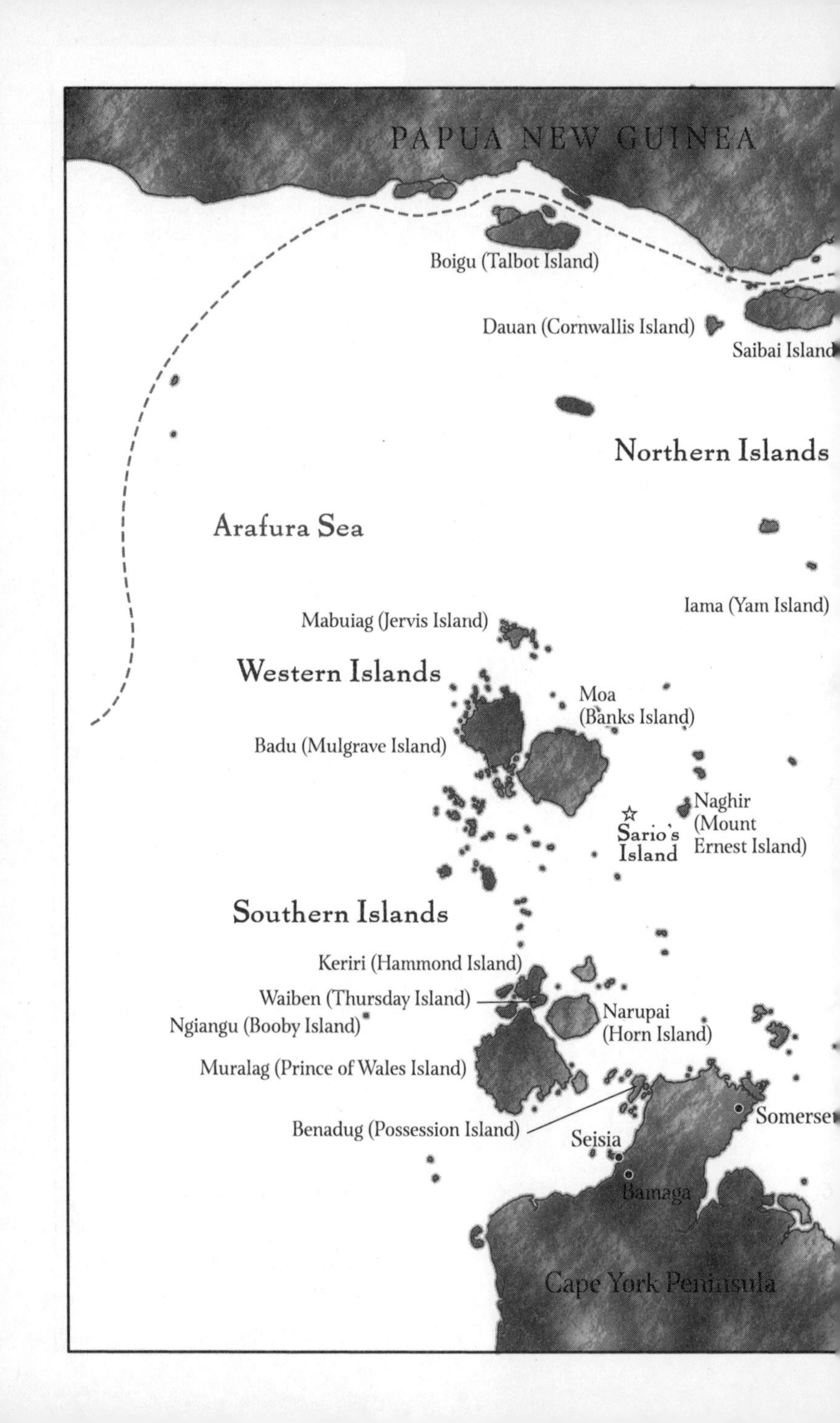
PAPUA NEW GUINEA
Boigu (Talbot Island)
Dauan (Cornwallis Island)
Saibai Island
Northern Islands
Arafura Sea
Iama (Yam Island)
Mabuiag (Jervis Island)
Western Islands
Moa
(Banks Island)
Badu (Mulgrave Island)
Naghir
(Mount
Ernest Island)
Sario's
Island
Southern Islands
Keriri (Hammond Island)
Waiben (Thursday Island)
Ngiangu (Booby Island)
Narupai
(Horn Island)
Muralag (Prince of Wales Island)
Benadug (Possession Island)
Seisia
Bamaga
Cape York Peninsula

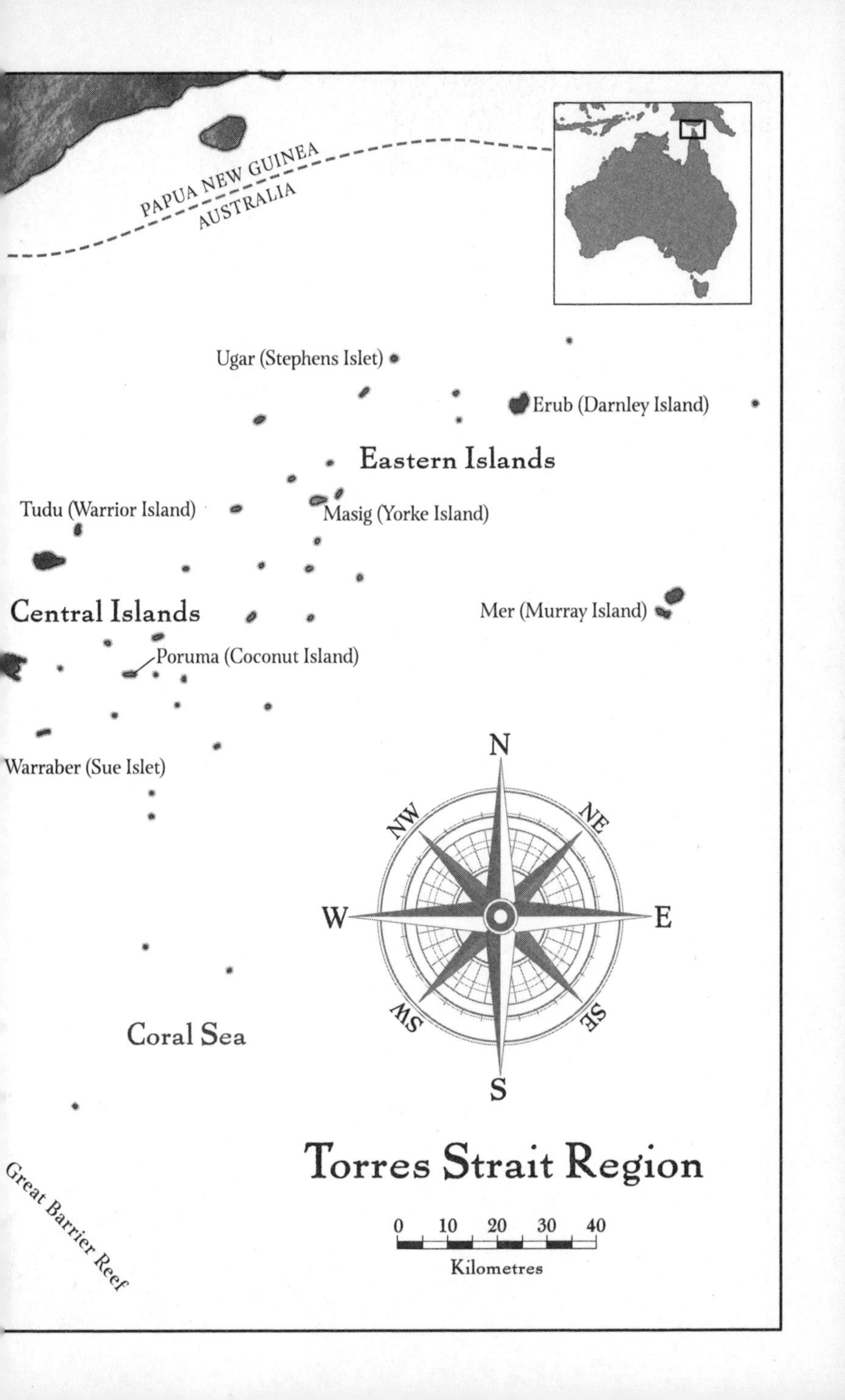
PAPUA NEW GUINEA
AUSTRALIA
Ugar (Stephens Islet)
Erub (Darnley Island)
Eastern Islands
Tudu (Warrior Island)
Masig (Yorke Island)
Central Islands
Mer (Murray Island)
Poruma (Coconut Island)
Warraber (Sue Islet)
N
NW
NE
W
E
SW
SE
S
Coral Sea
Torres Strait Region
Great Barrier Reef
0 10 20 30 40
Kilometres

Part One

~1898~

Chapter One

Sario shivers in the cool morning air as he leaves the hut. He darts through the coconut trees to ready the long canoe for fishing; the lull in the wind will not last long. He rubs at the goosebumps on his arms. Paddling will soon warm him up.

The first streaks of daylight are colouring the sky, but he can make out the nearby islands – dark lumps on the ocean – and see the whitecaps falling away. He peers out, his eyes drawn to a long shadowy shape bobbing in the distance: a pearling lugger. A shudder of unease ripples down his spine. The white man is back!

'*Markai!* Ghost man!' Esike confirms as he approaches. The lugger's high cabin and sharp hull are unmistakable as sunlight cuts across its deck.

Sario curls his toes into the cold, wet sand. He won't go with the ghost man. Never! The white man troubles him, his ghost-pale eyes always staring, always following him. Sario flings off the large mats covering the canoe with such force that he unsettles the sleepy fat lizards too.

'*Bal-nagi!* Turn and look!' Esike squeals.

Sario peers out as his young cousin dances around him with excitement. The pearling lugger is moving away, her white sails puffing out with wind. '*Uzari*, go!' He kicks at the wet sand and wills the lugger to go on, to keep sailing. 'Sail to Badu!' The island of Badu is far away – maybe the white man won't come back.

Esike picks up a handful of damp sand and smears his face white. He taps his chest. '*Markai*, whitefella.' He leaps forward, his eyes fierce, his jaw set, threatening. 'Get you, Sario!'

Sario laughs and ducks behind the long canoe, but inside he's tense, his nerves as tight as bowstrings. The white man will return! He knows it.

He watches Esike run into the sea and turns his attention back to the canoe. He can hear the clan coming, the soft whispering as they cross the sand carrying food and water. Many are old and weak, but he hopes for five or six strong paddlers. They'll travel far if the weather holds.

The aunties pass along food parcels wrapped in banana leaves and bamboo culms filled with drinking water, and the boys load the canoe. Sario stows coconuts and fishing twine and they push off into the deep. His uncle beckons him into the bow: 'Learn man's work!'

Sario jumps in after his father; Thaati will be proud to see how his skills have improved. He takes up a paddle and glances back at his island. Tall palm trees sway and seabirds peck, and the clear turquoise waters shimmer a sparkling ring around the white sands. His heart beats with connection, his link to his homeland.

The clan is soon pushing through the sea, grunting and heaving and finding rhythm with their paddles, water whooshing over the blades and the taste of salt on their tongues. Thaati scans the sea to the south and east, thankful for the lull in the high winds and rough seas.

Esike bursts out with his latest idea, his round face beaming. 'We gather plenty slugs and shells – exchange for big *guul*, sailing canoe.' The tribes of mainland New Guinea grow massive rainforest trees and hollow out long impressive canoes that travel far. 'Many paddlers.' He's counted thirty men in one canoe on the sea. They sail a long way to trade bird feathers and bamboo pipes.

Sario laughs at his foolish idea. 'Our clan is too small to paddle a big heavy *guul*.' Their canoe is not large, but it's a valuable possession and he sails it proudly to other islands to fish and trade. They'd been excited to find the log washed up on the beach – a lucky find, bigger than any hardwood tree they'd ever seen. The clan worked eagerly through two full moons to hollow it out, sharpening the bow and rounding the stern. He'd helped his cousins split long bamboo poles and lay a deck in the centre, wider than the canoe and lashed down crosswise with plaited vine. His uncles attached outrigger floats to each side to keep the canoe steady, and his aunties wove the large mat sails. Thaati cut the long steering pole at the back that sweeps them along on course.

Sario is hoping their next boat is a pearling lugger with tall masts and canvas sails. If the clan had their own lugger, their lives could stay the same. No one would need to leave the island and work for white men. They could pump-dive together and harvest their own pearl-shell. He'd stay and hunt the fat white pigeons with Esike and dig turtle eggs from the sand . . . everyone happy.

The wind picks up, and Sario helps Esike push the large mat sails up the bamboo poles. The sun is spreading its warm bright rays, and they can see other canoes dotting the green-blue ocean; some fishing with baits out on bamboo poles, others moving along, their mat sails puffed out with the freshening wind. Sario watches an old fishing lugger glide through the waves, its rigging draped with pearl-meat drying in the sun – a lucky catch for the dry-time. He sees crewmen asleep on the deck . . . could it be Kadub and Naku? His older cousins left on a white man's boat three rainy seasons ago, and they've never come back. Where are they now? No news filtered back, no money. Who could trust a white man? Island people are honest. If an Islander cheats, all trading with him will stop.

Sario listens to his wise uncle's instructions to study the sea: the sandbanks and reefs and sunken rocks. 'Map the *maalu*, sea, in your mind,' he says, his own eyesight poor now, and these waters not well known to them. Sario knows where dangerous reefs lie around his island; he's been diving since he was a small boy, learning from his uncles and Thaati. But now they have to travel much further to find enough sea-slugs and shells to trade – white men are wanting more and more.

His father points ahead to a rippling patch of sea, a sign of danger. They paddle closer to where a sharp spear of rock juts up, just below the surface. 'Look for a landmark – a sandbank or island,' Thaati instructs. Sario looks around for something to help him remember the rock's position, to fix it in his mind. The clan will warn others and pass on their knowledge. The currents are strong and unpredictable, and hazards are not easily seen – a dazzle of sunlight on the water's surface or a hazy mist can block a rock from view. Many boats lie wrecked on the bottom.

They find the reef, but it's still underwater. Thaati looks up at the sun. 'We wait – tide fall.' The reef will be exposed then, and they can dry-pick. 'No diving.' That way, the old ones will be able to collect shells with less effort and Leilani, his daughter, won't complain of sore ears.

Sario moves to the centre deck and helps his sister string up the wide shade mats. 'I'm proud of these *waku*,' Leilani says. She made the mats herself, splitting long pandanus leaves and weaving the strips into a tight pattern of squares. She grins at her younger brother; Sario is a clever diver, but she's a better weaver.

'*Kai kai*, food?' She hands him a banana-leaf parcel. '*Waru*, turtle? *Getalai*, crab? Yam?'

They sit together on the bamboo deck eating their food. She'll miss him if he goes and dives for the white man. '*Uzari markai?*' she asks.

Sario frowns and shakes his head. He wants to pump-dive more than anything, to go deep in a big breathing helmet and walk the sea-floor, but he won't go with the white man. He remembers his cousins leaving that grey rainy sunrise – Naku and Kadub swimming to the old pearling lugger, shouting and hollering and bubbling with adventure. 'Pump-dive,' they yelled. 'Earn white-fella money. Help clan.'

But they've never come back.

Chapter Two

The tide is low, the reef exposed. Sario leads the women barefoot over the sharp coral, their eyes keen for unbroken shell. His mother sings as she walks, her voice calming. She bends and picks up a large bailer shell. '*Kapu*, beautiful,' she cries. 'Good trade.'

The water is too cool for the big pink and white trochus cones with the snail inside; they like warm seas. They'll appear again when the slow monsoon tides return and pearl-shells are about. His auntie collects cowrie shells and puts them carefully in her net bag – she's hoping the mainland tribe will exchange her spotted brown shells for a fine *warup*, a drum with a lizard skin.

Sario squints into the sun, unsure if his eyes are playing tricks when he spots a patch of fat healthy sea-slugs. It's a lucky find – the white trader will take these long sea-slugs, bêche-de-mer, and sell them to China. He calls to Leilani, but his sister doesn't hear him and wanders on trailing her aunties, large seabirds squawking and diving around them. He can see the men off in the distance spearing fish, but he knows what to do. He'll collect the large fleshy slugs and leave the smaller ones to grow and mature. The white trader warns them often that Chinese buyers want undamaged slugs to cook in stews and soups and to use in medicines, so he's careful with the harvest. He lays the long cucumber slugs straight and flat in a drum of seawater and covers them with a mat.

When the tide washes back in, Sario stops collecting and heads back to the canoe. A few uncles and aunties are resting on the bamboo deck – it has been a long day of paddling and fishing for the old people. The small clan collected three bags of shells and two drums of sea-slugs, but it's not enough.

'Dive now,' Thaati says, when they've paddled on. He looks to the west where the sun is dipping; there's not a lot of daylight left for diving, but he'll take full advantage of the lull in the winds. He spots a shallow patch of coral and holds up his paddle. 'Stop here.' The sea is too cool for pearl-shell in the dry time, but they could be lucky.

The divers slip over the side, uncles and aunties and cousins, everyone except Leilani, who pulls at her ears. '*Kikiri*,' she says – her pain is worse when she dives deep. She stays in the canoe and watches the divers go down, young and old together, their bare bodies as slick as eels.

Sario stays on the leeward side of the reef, kicking down past blue-green parrot fish and yellow swaying coral, saltwater stinging his eyes. He moves quickly over the sea-bed, his toes feeling for hard shell; the water is murky, so it's difficult to see far. He grabs two shells and rises to the surface – one breath down and up.

His mother is back in the canoe. Apu looks ill, gasping and sucking in air as if every breath were her last. Older divers are climbing in too. Who's left diving? Sario looks around as heads bob up . . . a few uncles, an auntie, Esike, Thaati and himself. Is that all? This is a good patch of shell to find in the dry time, but he can see the old ones are tiring.

'Long day,' they complain. They've paddled a great distance, collected slugs and shells and dived as well, and still they have to paddle home. Sario sighs. What can he do? He's a quick diver with a sharp eye, but he can't carry the whole clan on his back. And a few more shells won't buy them a pearling lugger!

Thaati looks at his wife struggling to breathe, a worried frown crossing his forehead – she was forced to dive deep for too long as a girl, and now she suffers, her lungs damaged and weak. And the old ones are giving up as well. How much longer will the clan keep diving? What is their future? Can they harvest enough shell to buy white-man's tools and make their work on the island easier? And who will dive for pearl-shell when the calm seas return? They're short of divers with Leilani and Apu suffering, and the shell harvest is small after paddling so far. 'Last dive,' he shouts, his mind gloomy with his troubles.

Sario follows his father down, the light fading quickly with the sun dropping behind the islands. He spots a small shark nosing towards him as he reaches for another shell; dusk is feeding time on the reef, and they're a menace. He splashes and kicks and swirls the murky water and the shark swims on. Sario kicks quickly to the surface with a handful of shells. His clan cheer as he clambers into the canoe.

'Good diver.' Esike slaps his back. Sario always finds shell, even when there is little about and the water is murky and dangerous. Esike picks up his paddle and they turn the canoe for home. When he's older he'll be as slippery and quick as his cousin.

Sario spots birds ahead, diving and swooping. '*Wapi*, fish!' he calls. They paddle faster and scramble to throw in their fishing twine. The fish jump and splash and tug their lines. A large mackerel hooks up and Thaati pulls it in quickly. '*Buuzi* strong!' Sario shouts. He's twisted vines and made the fishing twine himself.

Sario hooks a large silver fish, but it leaps and tugs and fights his line for a long time. Then it bites through the vine and is gone. 'Oww!' he wails, his palms cut and bleeding from the running line. The big fish played him a long time and still he's lost it. And it's taken his turtle-shell hook! He dips his hands in the seawater and scrunches his face with the sting of salt and disappointment.

Esike aims his spear and throws, leaping into the sea along with it. He pierces a big silver fish between the gills.

'Is it the same *wapi*?' Sario scans the fish for his hook as Esike swims back with it flapping on his spear. '*Launga*, no,' he mutters.

Leilani takes Sario's hands in hers and examines his cuts. '*Kikiri*, pain,' she cries, drawing her lips in at the sight of his oozing raw flesh. She will heal his stinging palms, she assures him. She's made a new soothing balm from banana.

But Sario doesn't answer, still annoyed with himself for losing the big mackerel and his turtle-shell hook.

'No matter, *babat*.' Her brother is a clever diver, even the white trader knows it and wants him in his crew. 'Good harvest. Lucky *guul*,' she says, smiling and trying to cheer him up.

Sario picks up his paddle and scans the sea, his hands throbbing. He's pleased that they've found pearl-shells in the dry-time and a healthy batch of sea-slugs, but the clan needs bigger harvests – more shells to trade.

He tenses suddenly and stares ahead at a boat bobbing in the distance. '*Markai?*' His gaze moves over the pearling lugger, his skin prickling with dread. It's too dark to see clearly. He scans the hull again . . . it's shorter than the white man's boat. He sighs with relief and pushes up the mat sails.

The men navigate home by the stars of Tagai, the Southern Cross, guiding their direction. Thaati points to the night sky. 'See Tagai standing in his *guul*, the stars in line; his warrior's spear in his left hand.'

Sario listens to his father's story of how the mighty warrior Tagai became part of the huge constellation in the sky. 'Tagai went fishing with twelve crewmen. He took water and *kai kai* for the voyage. While he searched the reef for fish, his crew became hungry and thirsty. They ate all the *kai kai* and drank all the water. Tagai was so angry he shook with rage; he'd been on the reef a long time without food and drink. He strung up his crew – two groups of six. They rose into the sky and became stars.'

Apu nods and says in short sharp breaths, 'Tagai guides our people on the land so we know when to hunt and plant crops.' Her voice fades to a whisper. 'Rest now.' She sighs and closes her eyes.

Sario yawns; he needs his sleep too. But it isn't long before he sees the jagged peaks of his island, the dark band of trees and creeper vines, and the rows of palm trees along the beach bending to the sea. Beyond the sand, a shimmer of moonlight lights the thatched huts. 'B'long here,' he mutters. This is his home, his link to his ancestors, his spirit.

He'll stay here forever.

Chapter Three

Leilani wakes early. There is much work to do with the harvest, but first she'll find Sario and examine the cuts on his hands. '*Dawa* is good,' she says, nodding and smiling; her banana balm is healing his wounds nicely. She smears another layer over his palms and hurries to tell her aunties. '*Gabun-mai!*' she calls with pride – she can heal! She'll make a remedy for Apu and help her breathing!

The aunties spread woven mats on the sand, and sit to prepare the oyster shells for trade. Leilani opens a pearl-shell carefully, slipping the tip of her sharp bamboo knife into a slit between the lips and twisting to break the shell apart. She digs out the oyster flesh and hangs the meat to dry in the sun, then scrubs the shell halves clean in seawater. '*Kapu*, beautiful!' she cries, holding them up to the sunlight. The pearl-oyster's shell is plain and crusty on the outside, but inside it dazzles with beauty. The hard glossy nacre lining shimmers a rainbow of colour – mother-of-pearl.

Sario and Esike gather dry mangrove sticks and build a fire on the beach to cook the bêche-de-mer. Esike sorts the long sea-slugs and Sario cuts them carefully along the upper side, his knife sharp and each slit short and straight and wide enough to fit three fingers. He pulls out the guts and squeezes along the fleshy cucumber bodies, emptying them of sand and water.

Esike picks up the slimy guts. '*Gasamai*, catch!' He throws the muck at Sario, and runs away laughing.

Sario grabs his cousin at the water's edge and tussles him to the sand. He rubs the smelly guts through Esike's black curls and down his face. They giggle and wrestle and roll into the waves, exhausted.

The fire has died down and is ready for cooking. Sario slips the slugs into a pot of seawater and stirs them with a bamboo stick. When the slugs are firm, he lifts them out and rolls them in salt and places them on a rack to dry, spacing and sloping them so that all moisture can drain away.

It's a long process cooking and drying the slugs over three sunrises, but if the quality is good, traders will come back and buy again. The white man says buyers in faraway China will pay a high price for quality bêche-de-mer.

'*Mui* not too hot,' Sario warns as he chooses the slugs he'll smoke over the smouldering fire. 'No strong smell of *tu*, smoke.' They'll boil the slugs again until the skin becomes thick, lay them out in the sun to dry, then pack them in sacks.

Thaati wanders up the beach calling to the clan resting under the shady beach-almond tree. 'Look at my catch of *getalai*.' He laughs and holds up his fistful of mud crabs. The choppy, breezy conditions have subsided, and the sea has settled again. '*Maalu* calm,' he says. 'We should be gathering more shell, not working to clean and bag our catch.' He suggests they take their slugs and shells to a shore-station for processing next time. 'Let other *mabaegal*, men, do the cleaning and sorting.'

The elders wriggle about restlessly. No one wants change. 'Will other *mabaegal* process as carefully as we do?' an uncle asks. 'Will they pay us for the whole catch?'

'If we fish longer our catches will be better,' Thaati argues. 'More to trade. More money to buy tools.'

Sario glares at his father. He's asking them to hand over their harvest? White men are a bad lot – how could they trust the white-man boss at the shelling station? He's heard about white men who raid islands and steal taro and fruit from the gardens. Men who force small children to dive for shell, then pay them with sweets and keep the money for themselves. Men who take young divers away and never let them return to their islands. 'Some *markai* can't be trusted, Thaati,' he warns. 'They don't deserve our respect.' He wants to be free of white men! The station boss could easily cheat them; white-man cash is still new to his clan. They've never needed money, they exchange everything – spears and crops, bows and arrows, shells and feathers. Island trading is all they know.

His father raises his eyebrows, shocked at Sario's outburst. But his son is growing up and has a right to speak his mind. 'Not *all markai* can be trusted,' he agrees. Since white men have taken control of the islands, there has been less freedom and more rules. 'Protectors interfere with our culture, but they offer opportunities,' Thaati adds. 'We should learn from them and look beyond our *kaiwa*, island.'

Sario stiffens. He doesn't want to know what's beyond his island, he's happy here. 'Some *markai* cruel men, Thaati,' he argues. 'They're punishing divers for no reason.' He's heard the talk, how pearl-shell boys work hard for their bosses and white men treat them bad. 'No money, little *kai kai*, and no time to fish. A *mabaeg* needs food in his belly to dive!'

Thaati nods, proud to hear his son yarning in English; he encourages white-talk. He wants the boys to trade with white men and understand their culture, to be more confident and not cower away. But his wife is trembling, her head filled with bad memories from when she was a small girl – being forced to dive when she was cold and hungry, her head held underwater.

'We must harvest more shell and take advantage of the progress,' Thaati goes on. 'Torres Strait is a busy shipping route. Traders are coming from all places.'

'*Markai* make the rules!' Sario blurts. He stands and heads for the palm trees to collect coconuts. 'Islanders have no say.'

He sees the pearling boat and draws back behind the coconut trees, digging his toes into the sand. The white man's sleek lugger is tugging at its anchor in the deep water. The *markai* is rowing towards the island.

Sario watches him drag his dinghy up onto the sand and lift out a heavy brown sack. He hears him call, seeking permission to come onto the land.

His father answers, welcoming the trader to come and buy shell, exchange goods.

Sario winds through the coconut trees, out of sight, trailing the ghost-coloured man up the beach. What has he brought? Knives? Axes? Cooking pots? He hears the *clink-clink* of metal as the white man walks, his weighty sack slapping against his legs. Sario waits for his father to greet the tall trader and offer him a drink, then he steps out – Thaati will keep him safe.

The man raises his straw hat and mops his ruddy face. 'Knives? Tobacco? Cloth? Everything you need!' He lays his goods out along the yarning log. 'What do you have for me today? Pearl-shell? Bêche-de-mer? I've been sailing the Strait collecting carved curiosities and I'll take all the turtle-shell you have.' He eyes the dark-skinned clan gathering around and accepts a coconut with the top lopped off. He drinks slowly, allowing his gaze to linger on the boy. He's grown since his last visit – wider shoulders, broader chest. Thirteen, fourteen? Just right for his crew.

Sario twitches, sensing the ghost man watching. It's disrespectful! He should go, avoid the man's pale staring eyes. But a big shiny knife has his attention, its silver blade glinting in the sunlight, winking and drawing him in. He picks it up. It's heavy, with a thick wooden handle and long smooth blade. He slices the air – sharp and swift as a sailor's cutlass. It would slash bamboo and chop thick vines with one sweep.

'You like the machete, boy?' A heavy hand clamps down on his head, flattening his springy curls. 'Dive with me and you can have it.'

Sario jerks and twists, but the pressure increases. The trader's long fingers crawl over his scalp, squeezing and releasing . . . squeezing and releasing. Sario raises the blade, his head throbbing, pulsing.

Esike draws in a breath. His heart is racing. '*Launga*, no!'

Thaati steps forward, his jaw tight; his eyes fierce with warning.

Sario lets the knife fall to his side. White men have to be respected, and the trader is important. He'd be punished. Shamed. Bring disgrace to his clan. But the ghost man has a crooked streak . . . a dishonest undercurrent. Can't Thaati feel it? The tall man looks trustworthy – his shirt buttoned neatly, his smile friendly, looking as smart and sharp as his lugger – but underneath lies an evil spirit, more dangerous than a wreck under water. Can't the elders sense it? Sario lets the knife swing slowly, back and forth, back and forth.

'How old are you now, boy? Thirteen? Fourteen?'

Sario's head whips back. His neck cracks. He closes his eyes tight, shutting out the ghost-pale face, the stink of stale tobacco.

'Old enough to earn a wage for your elderly uncles, don't you think?'

The trader's voice is jovial and matey, but his manner is pushy, bullying. He smiles at the elders. 'What do you think, men?' They'll want the cash to buy tools and gadgets, he knows – darkies are the same everywhere. 'You'd like that, wouldn't you, boy – sailing the seas in my majestic lugger?' He waits, expecting the boy's eyes to light up with interest.

Sario squirms. He feels the tug of enticement – of course he does. He dreams of sailing in a pearling lugger and pump-diving the ocean in a helmet and suit. But he won't go with a white man, he won't leave his family and homeland. He might never come back!

His father understands the offer. The trader is asking to take his son away to dive for pearl-shell. It's not unusual; many children go and work on boats, and Sario is a strong swimmer and a good diver. Any white skipper would want him. And in return, the clan would get money – white-man's cash. Sario's pay would allow them to purchase tools from the cargo boats, hatchets and spades. But he churns with indecision. If Sario goes, who will dive for their catch? The clan is small; some are too young and many are old and weak, they cannot raise enough shell without him. And what has happened to Kadub and Naku? Are they working for greedy white men who keep their pay and treat them bad? Thaati paces, his thinking confused. He could lose Sario, his only son. But does he have a choice?

The elders yarn in anxious whispers. They have a dilemma. They don't want white-man trouble. The trader wields great power through the islands and his reputation as a scheming *markai* who gets his own way is well known. But if they let Sario go, how will they manage their harvesting? No one else can dive as deep or raise as much pearl-shell.

Leilani spots a length of cloth and steps forward to feel it. It is strong cotton. '*Pagami*, sew,' she pleads with her father. She could make two long dresses from it – one for herself and one for Apu. Her mother's dresses are worn and torn. And when the missionaries came with their Bibles and books and church lessons, didn't they say she must cover up more? That she must act ladylike now she's fourteen? *It's indecent to expose your body, Leilani. Cover your breasts. Discard your short leaf petticoat. You are a young Christian woman. Sew yourself a pretty long dress and cover your ankles.*

Thaati shakes his head and raises his eyebrows. For his daughter to have cloth and trinkets, they'd need to dive deeper and harvest more shell. Is the clan willing to paddle longer distances and find new shell-beds? Harvest more slugs?

The trader notices the girl's disappointment. 'We barter for the cloth. Bring me all your shells. Everything.' He looks around at the other women. 'You want flour, missus? Rice? Tea? I have plenty sugar in my lugger.'

Sario wriggles, but the *markai*'s bony fingers press deeper. 'You want to earn money, boy? Help your clan?'

Thaati points to the full sacks of sea-slugs to distract the trader. 'Bêche-de-mer? Smoked? Boiled?'

The trader's eyes skim the sacks stacked under the bamboo shelter and return to Sario. 'You want the shiny machete, boy?' He tightens his grip. 'How deep do you dive?'

Sario concentrates on a gull, watching it flap its wings and lift off . . . if he were a bird, he'd fly out of the white man's clutches.

'You read weather patterns? The wind and clouds?' The trader feels the boy resisting, but he needs him, a healthy strong boy with a good knowledge of the sea. He's heard talk of his diving ability.

The men haul the sacks of slugs and shells to the yarning log. 'We have big feast to prepare,' an uncle says. If Sario can hold the trader's attention, bartering could work in their favour.

But Thaati's had enough of the trader manhandling his son; he wants him to exchange goods and get off their island. He steps up to the white man, his chest bared, his chin out. The elders quickly close in, warning Thaati to back off, avoid trouble, consider the consequences.

'*Wakain-tamai*, think!' There will be white-man payback. They wave him away.

The aunties move in to help calm the situation, yarning and pointing to goods they want in exchange for the harvest. Flour. Tea. Biscuits. As much as they can get for their feast.

'Ah yes, it's almost July,' the trader says. 'Time for your Coming of the Light celebrations.' He prods Sario's chest with his finger. 'After the festivities, you will be coming to dive on my lugger.' He shoves him away and turns to the clan to barter.

Sario puts the shiny knife on the log and flees to the rocks, his heart thumping, his feet flying across the sand. He gathers periwinkles and smashes them on the boulders, his mind racing, making plans.

Chapter Four

He moves through the coconut palms gathering the nuts that have fallen to the ground. If that sharp machete were his he could lop whole bunches in one swoop. He'd slash down banana trunks, he'd chop bamboo fishing poles; he'd take that shiny knife everywhere. Sario slams the big coconuts into a large woven basket. *Boom. Boom. Boom.* Why is the white trader pestering him? Why can't he take other island boys, other divers? He isn't going with him . . . machete or not!

Sario drags the basket across the sandy dirt to where a sharp wooden spike pokes up from the ground, waist-high. The trader is still yarning with Thaati. Why are they looking his way? He's not for trade! He's not a sack of goods to barter. Sario grabs a big nut and slams it down hard on the sharp wooden spike. *Crrr-ack!* He tears away the thick outer husk, stripping away wads of dry yellowy fibre until nothing remains except the small hairy coconut inside.

Esike approaches. He's never seen his cousin so angry. 'Rip that trader apart,' he says, practising his white-talk. 'Get mad at that coconut-head.' He passes Sario another big nut and takes away the small brown one. He doesn't want his cousin to leave the island like Kadub and Naku. No one does – this is their home, their paradise.

Sario slams the big nuts down on the sharp spike and cracks them open as if every one is the trader's head. Esike gathers the dry husks and tosses them into the basket – they'll use them later in the fire. He stacks the small husked nuts on top, and drags the basket to the yarning log.

Sario strides off to the open bamboo kitchen with its breezy palm-leaf roof, where his mother and aunties are singing and preparing food. He collects two woven baskets, two large cockle-shell scrapers and a cooking pot. The trader is rowing away from the island, and Sario is pleased to see the back of him . . . but he wishes he'd left his shiny machete.

Esike whacks the small brown nuts with a knife and splits them open. He tips the milky coconut water into the cooking pot and sits with Sario on the yarning log to scrape out the white flesh. Sario scrapes furiously, grinding the hard flesh away with frustration until every shell is empty and crumbs of white coconut lie in the basket between his knees. The clan need their own lugger – could they barter for a pearling boat? Not without white-man's money!

He'll plant more coconut trees. He'll extract the oil and sell it. He'd need a large plantation . . . plenty of palm trees.

He ponders the idea as he carries the baskets to the kitchen. How long to grow a plantation? How long to extract enough coconut oil to buy a boat? A long, long time – he'll be an old man before it happens!

He drops the baskets of shredded coconut on the sandy ground beside his mother. Apu is peeling and chopping pumpkin and sweet potato to boil over the fire. He sways to her music; her singing is comforting and familiar from deep in her belly, but she is struggling for every breath now – he can hear her shallow gasps.

She tips the shredded coconut into a bowl and pours a little water over it. She shows Leilani how to squeeze the coconut with her hands. 'The first squeeze makes cream.' Apu sets the cream aside and continues her instructions. 'When pumpkin and *kumala*, sweet potato, cooked, drain and pour in coconut milk, then *dawa* and salt. Cream last.' Leilani needs to practise and become confident cooking *sop sop*.

Sario licks his lips and leaves the kitchen, his mouth ready for the delicious *sop sop*. He picks up his fishing spear and calls to Esike. '*Wapi?* Come fishing?'

His mother's singing is faint now; he can no longer hear her hymns from the fishing rocks, the songs she sang when she scooped water from the spring and dug new gardens and planted yams and picked bananas – the songs he hopes she will never stop singing.

The water is rising, the tide high. Esike climbs a big smooth boulder and spots fish below. He aims his spear at a blue-green parrot fish and throws. He misses. He tosses Sario a wad of coconut husk. 'Chew. Make berley.'

Sario chews and spits the soggy fibre into the water. They watch as small fish splash to the surface, bait-size, just right for their hooks. Esike scoops them in his net.

They hook and spear and gut and clean, and by sundown their catch is roasting in the coals. They laze on the sand and watch a ship pass by, her tall funnels puffing smoke. 'Waiben far away,' Esike says. Thursday Island is a long way south, but he'd like to visit the whitefella island. '*Uzari*, go?' Sario has the chance to see it.

Sario glares back at Esike, puzzled by his cousin's change of thinking. '*Launga*, no!' He's not leaving his homeland, he's not going anywhere!

'*Markai* take you.' Esike ponders the opportunity to sail in a lugger and see steamships loading coal and houses with glass windows and stores trading fish hooks – everything they've heard about. 'Big gun on the shore. *Boom!*'

'*Launga!*' Sario sets out the fish bones he'll sharpen into arrowheads and the broken shells he'll shape into hooks. He spreads mats for his aunties and uncles and cousins to join them by the fire.

The women bring taro and sweet potato from the garden to cook with the fish, and Leilani places a new vegetable in the coals.

'Makem corn,' she says when it's cooked. She pushes the strange new vegetable around in her mouth. It isn't island food, but with tender care she got the plant to grow.

'Mmmm.' Thaati likes the taste of the corn. A sailor gave him the plant after he helped him mend a broken mast. 'Soil not so rich here,' Thaati says, and tells the story of Gelam and why their island is not as fertile as those in the east. 'Gelam and his mother lived on Moa,' he says. 'Gelam had a disagreement with his mother, so he carved a log in the shape of a *dhangal*, dugong, and swam away. He swam all the way to Mer and took all the rich soil and plant seeds from Moa inside the *dhangal* and gave the gifts to Mer. Now that island grows the best yams and fruit plants. He buried himself on Mer, and forms a big hill in the shape of a *dhangal*.'

'No matter, Leilani,' an auntie says, tasting the new food from the coals. 'Your corn grow good.'

They sit in their yarning circle, everyone listening to the elders tell stories and teach right from wrong, values and lessons to guide them through life. Leilani sits cross-legged, a bright yellow flower in her hair, threading small shells and seeds onto vine to make a pretty necklace. She knots the twine around her neck, and the pearl-shell at the centre shimmers against her dark skin.

Thaati puts down the fishing net he's weaving and stands. 'Men of every skin colour stop here to collect firewood and water,' he says. 'We must show respect and encourage them to trade and exchange shell.'

Sario watches his father pace about the sand, his face tense in the firelight. He knows more difficult words are coming.

'Next time the trader comes, you go with him, Sario. Dive for pearl-shell and learn the *markai*'s ways.' Thaati looks away; it upsets him to say it, but the elders have made the decision. '*Uzari*. Earn money.'

'You strong diver, Sario. Help clan,' an elder adds. 'Esike will soon take your place, he's diving deeper and growing quickly, getting stronger. We be alright.'

Sario swallows, unable to form words. What are they saying? Leave his island? Leave his family? Have they forgotten Naku and Kadub? He looks around his clan, at his mother and Leilani, his aunties and cousins, their sad eyes filling with tears. No one is yarning or speaking for him. The elders have decided.

'It's your dream to pump-dive, Sario,' his uncle says. 'Work hard – you get the chance.'

Sario argues. 'We get an island lugger and pump-dive together. No one has to go away.' It sounds foolish when he says it. How could they buy a pearling lugger? They can't even harvest enough shell to buy cloth!

His uncle grins. 'Money b'long whitefella.'

Thaati is torn, but all he can do is encourage his son. 'White man pay you well, Sario. You good diver, strong and clever, no harm come to you.' If Sario dives for the white man, they will have money to buy kerosene and axes; if Sario refuses, the white man will pursue him and make trading difficult.

'White-man's cash, we buy tools,' an elder says.

Sario's mind clogs like a net full of seaweed. If he goes with the white man he'll earn money and help his clan. He'll get the machete. He'll sail in a lugger and learn to pump-dive. But how can he trust the white man? Would the trader pay up? Send the money to the clan? Bring him back to see his family?

'Soon you be a *mabaeg*, Sario. Time to spread your wings and fly like a bird,' his wise uncle says. 'We be here when you return.'

Sario snatches up his fishhooks and leaves the circle. 'B'long here!'

He rolls out his sleeping mat and curls into his thoughts. At sunrise they will go and fish for the big feast, and everyone will forget the white-man trader.

Chapter Five

'Sario.' Esike's voice comes to him through a sleepy fog. '*Maalu* calm.'

Sario shakes himself awake, his thoughts a jumble and his heart heavy. Thaati's words keep repeating in his head, dragging him down like an anchor, but he has to stay alert and hunt for the feast – the Coming of the Light is serious business.

He hears the hollers of excitement coming from the beach, the men itching to get on the sea and fish – they've readied the canoe without him. They cheer when Sario arrives carrying his harpoon and spears. Esike splashes him with seawater. 'Wake up! Many visitors coming for *kai kai*.'

'Spear big *waru*, turtle,' Apu calls to her son. 'Good hunter, Sario!'

Whoops of joy ring out from the aunties as they follow the well-beaten path to the gardens. Leilani picks a flower for her hair and leads her excited aunties to the fruit trees. They shout orders over the crowing rooster. 'Pick this paw-paw and those *dawa*, the ripest fruit. Dig up taro and cassava.' They make plans to tidy and prepare the village; it's a busy day ahead. 'Sweep *butu*,' an auntie says; she'll place clamshells in a neat pattern in the swept sand to lead the visitors in. The little girls run off excitedly to make a new palm-leaf broom, and the older ones agree to wash and polish the big bailer shells ready for serving *sop sop*.

The men scan the sea, waiting for a small turtle head to break the calm surface. Sario stands in the bow of the canoe, his special harpoon ready, its bamboo prongs sharp. A carved wooden head looks out from the prow, its large painted eyes trained on the waterline. Sario shooshes the men as a turtle rises and splutters to the surface, a *waru* as long as his paddle!

His spear strikes the hard shell and bounces off, and the turtle goes under. Esike throws a line quickly; the long vine has a sucker-fish attached, which fastens onto the turtle and goes down with it. The canoe follows along on the surface, the crew tracking the turtle's movements below, its greeny-brown colour fading as it goes deeper.

Sario balances himself in the bow, waiting for the turtle to rise again and break the surface. The water parts. He raises his harpoon and throws. The barb strikes and the turtle dives, Esike paying out a long line as it goes deeper and deeper, until he feels the line slacken and the turtle giving up, too tired to fight.

The men haul the heavy turtle into the canoe, flipping it belly-up, its soft flesh for all to see. 'Look big-eye to the feast,' Sario says, licking his lips at the thought of hot turtle meat from the ground-oven, served with taro and mangrove shoots. His aunties will boil squid and clams and cook rice; they'll gather taro and sweet potato from the garden, roasting some in the ashes of the fire and simmering some in milky coconut water. Apu will cook damper, and he'll dip it in his *sop sop*. The feast is always delicious, with everyone welcome. Later he will polish the turtle's pretty shell, the colour of dry bush, and ready it for trade.

The big mat sail catches the breeze and the bow cuts through the smooth sea towards home. The men cheer, reliving the thrill of their hunt. Underwater reefs are difficult to see when the sun is high in the sky, but Sario is mapping as many hazards in his mind as he can: the coral reef where they speared the red trout, the small mangrove island alive with mud crabs, the sandbank that is hidden until the tide falls.

Sario spots a patch of clipped sea-grass as they glide into their shallow turquoise bay. He whispers to the men that a dugong is feeding and scans the calm sea – a big dugong would feed the clan and visitors many times over, its meat tender and rich in oil. 'Good *kai kai*!'

They hear the blow behind them, a deep sighing sound as a massive dugong surfaces and expels air before diving again quickly to the safety of the deep. 'We wait – *dhangal* will feed again,' Sario says, and readies his harpoon. A good hunter is patient.

In the distance he can see the clan moving about the island carrying baskets of food and preparing for the feast. Apu will be mixing flour with water and kneading lumps of dough into damper. Leilani will be chopping pumpkin and sweet potato and making delicious *sop sop* with coconut cream. His aunties will be gathering wood for the fire and waiting to boil the fresh catch of prawns and crabs.

'*Ssshhh!*' The big barrel body of the dugong is there suddenly, under the canoe, its wide grey snout feeding on the sea-grass. Sario crouches and silently raises his spear – a dugong is sensitive to sound, just a drip from a paddle could scare it away.

He leaps. His spear strikes. Everyone's alert. 'Don't lose *dhangal*,' the men shout. Esike loops its fluked tail and the dugong takes off out to sea, the vine uncoiling. 'Hold him,' the men shout, the vine pulling tight. When the line slackens, they haul the massive dugong in to the beach, the sun slipping low in the sky behind them. Sario puts the conch shell to his lips and blows, its deep mellow sound announcing the proud hunters' catch.

'*Gorsar*, plenty!' Esike calls to his aunties on the beach, his smile beaming. They have a full canoe. '*Getalai, waru, dhangal.*'

Everyone laughs and chatters and carries the catch from the canoe, the aunties anxious to chop off the fish heads and make soup. He'll suck every bit of flesh from the bones, Sario decides, his belly rumbling.

The men set about carving up the catch, cutting the turtle from its shell and slicing the dugong's fleshy meat. Leilani watches the oil ooze from the dugong as she sits plaiting palm leaves into small neat boxes to hold the rice. 'Rich *idi*,' she says; she'll use the precious oil in her healing balm.

Long canoes are arriving from nearby islands and being tied together in the mangroves. Friendly neighbours are handing over baskets of food and gifts – mats and masks and medicine plants, and a wild pig lashed to a bamboo pole, ready to butcher. Shrieks of excitement fill the air as the visitors are welcomed.

The men are soon cutting the pig into joints and rubbing the meat with salt. The women are wrapping the meat in banana leaves, along with the dugong and fish and chickens, and large parcels of freshly dug vegetables. There are plenty of visitors to help. Young boys are digging and preparing the ground-oven, and some are using white-man's spades to make their work easier.

The elders enjoy the extra help and yarn about the boys' sturdy iron spades. Perhaps they can purchase some of these strong white-man tools before the next drytime arrives.

Sario moves away with a shiver of guilt, but quickly pushes off any thoughts and concerns. He's not leaving his *kaiwa*, the clan need him here to harvest the catch. Let the *markai* take other island boys!

The men pile dry grass, wood and large stones into the hole in the sand, and start a fire. When the stones are red hot and the fire has died, they make a well and lay in the parcels of food. They cover the hole with branches and coconut leaves, then spread wet mats and shovel sand and dirt on top.

The handclapping and singing starts and festivities begin. Barefoot dancers thud over the sand, their bodies moving to the deep beat of the drum, their grass skirts swishing gracefully; their feet stamping the ground. The men advance in a wave, then fall back, telling of the wind that blows strongly, then dies away. Sario watches boys his age do the shake-a-leg dance. Are they quick, strong divers like him? Would they leave their island and dive for white men?

Men wear pale masks in the dance of the ghost ships, the first sighting of white men in sailing ships; their feet move in unison, short palm leaves tied to their ankles. Women clap and rattle seed-shakers, their high-pitched voices singing ancient songs about the wind and tides and fishing canoes.

Sario watches his uncles surge forward, raising one foot at a time in a slow step like seagulls, their faces fierce and determined. They wear woven armbands and arch-shaped headdresses curving down around their faces, the crisp white feathers plucked from long-legged wading herons.

Pearl-shells shimmer around their necks and Sario's heart beats with pride.

He follows the swish of grass skirts as the procession moves to the shore, gentle waves breaking around them and smells of meat roasting in the air. The men demonstrate how Christian missionaries landed on the islands of the Torres Strait, re-enacting their peaceful arrival with their Bibles and teachings. How they calmed the wild fighting men and brought hope to the hostile tribes. How the clans accepted their friendship and shared their values and put down their warrior spears.

The solemn group move back up the beach. 'The spirits are happy we celebrate this day,' an elder says. 'No more warrior raids. No enemy islands. We gather together safely. Head-hunting days are over.'

After the dancing and re-enactment everyone is hungry, the women breaking into whoops of joy as the men shovel away dirt and open the ground-oven. They carry the steaming food parcels to the big mats and serve the prawns and crab meat on banana leaves. Everyone bows their head and thanks their God.

Men continue to yarn about their history, how the Torres Strait people became Christians.

'When clans were fighting there was no hope,' a visitor says. 'Small clans would have wiped each other out unless they'd put down their weapons. No man was sure of his life. Missionaries brought law and order and offered protection. They taught us about the world and we saw the light.'

'The missionaries brought hope, but they destroyed our sacred objects and changed our traditions,' Thaati says. 'Much of our culture is lost. It's a white-man's world now.'

As the feasting and celebrating finishes and the last hymns of praise are ringing out, Sario joins other boys in a dance of farewell, their grass skirts moving in waves.

Now the festivities are over, his thoughts are returning to the white man. '*Markai* is our enemy now,' he tells Esike on their way to the huts. 'When trader comes, I hide.'

'Where?'

Sario shakes his head, he doesn't know. 'I make plans.'

Esike laughs. 'Small island, Sario. How you disappear?'

Sario considers this as he wanders to his hut.

'Big trouble!' Esike warns.

Chapter Six

Sario wakes to a thundering sound he's never heard before. He leaps to his feet. It isn't the surf breaking on the reef. It isn't the sky rumbling. Is it rocks tumbling? Is his island breaking up?

Animals! The biggest four-legged beasts he's ever seen. Bigger than wild goats, bigger than bristly pigs. He grips the hut's bamboo post as they thunder up the beach, their heavy feet spraying sand and their long hair flying. They bolt past in a blur of colour, and up into the hills.

Thaati runs through the village waving his arms. 'Bring *buuzi*. Catch them.'

Sario grabs a coil of fishing vine and follows the men. The massive beasts are running amok in the gardens, trampling the food crops with their hard bony feet. 'Stop!' cries an auntie. 'Garden be gone!'

How can they stop them? The giant hairy monsters are stomping and snorting and ripping out leafy green vegetables, tossing back their heads and wolfing down the bananas, showing their big brown teeth. Two beasts gallop past him to the spring, feet thudding and noses stretched, sniffing fresh water. Sario leaps for his life, his ears ringing with their loud whinnies – louder than any ship's foghorn!

Thaati snatches a length of twine and makes a loop. He tosses it over the neck of a pony, too exhausted to be flighty after its long swim. He leads it to a tree and ties it to the trunk. Sario fetches an empty drum and approaches the spring cautiously to fill it. The pony watches from the tree, its big eyes on the drum as Sario comes closer. It whinnies suddenly and tosses its head. It's so close and scary Sario shakes and sloshes water down his legs. He dumps the drum and runs for his life.

He hands out lengths of vine to his uncles; there are still six beasts to be caught. He hears a faint whistle and turns. Apu is pointing at a pony, its head down eating. 'Sneak up,' she mouths, moving her fingers forward as if walking.

Sario loops his vine and edges closer, his hands trembling. The beast lifts its head and chews, its huge mouth green from the vegetables. He tosses the rope and rings its neck. It rears, striking out with its long legs, its eyes wild, ears flat. He backs away, the twine slipping through his fingers, the hard hooves kicking dangerously close.

Apu hurries to grab the vine and hold the flighty beast. It bucks and kicks and froths at the mouth, stretching its neck and trying to break the restraint, but the vine is strong. The more the wild brown pony fights and pulls, the deeper the vine cuts into its neck, but they persist, whispering and calming it gently. When it settles, they fasten the pony to a shady tree, beside two others who are sniping and tugging at their vines. The pony dunks its head in the drum and drinks deeply. How long will the beasts stay there together? They'll chew through the vine, their teeth are so big!

Sario spots another pony in Leilani's new corn patch, its coat creamy-white, the colour of sand. He steps closer. How will he catch it now all the vine has gone?

He hears a voice: white-talk. 'Grab it around the neck.'

The white trader? Sario stiffens. His heart is beating like a drum. If he runs, he'll startle the beast and it will gallop into the hills. If he does nothing it will destroy the whole crop! He turns slowly . . .

It isn't the tall white trader. It's a short white man, a sailor, his trousers rolled up, his shirt loose and unbuttoned.

'*Sshhh!*' The sailor puts his finger to his lips and holds up a rope. He signals Sario to sneak up quietly and circle the pony's neck with his arms. 'Hold it until I can rope it.'

Sario trembles. The man wants him to hang from its neck? He's seen its huge teeth and bone-hard feet.

'Hurry!' the sailor urges.

Sario steps out, his legs wobbling under him. He's never been so close to an animal so big and dangerous.

The pony looks up, aware he is near but too hungry to leave the corn. Sario follows the sailor's instructions, holding out his hand to let the animal sniff him, trembling under its hot heavy breath with its strong, grassy smell. '*Sshhh*,' he whispers, stepping closer and reaching out to touch the beast. He feels its muscles twitch as he slides his hand slowly up the sweaty pulsing neck and through its thick hairy mane.

'Hold him, boy.' The sailor tosses the rope and Sario slips the large loop quickly over the pony's twitching ears and down its long nose. The beast snorts and Sario leaps back.

'Well done. Good job!' The sailor smiles.

Sario stares at the man – his hair is so red he can't look away. And his skin is blotchy and pink from the sun, spotty like a cod!

'We ran aground in fog this morning. The ship hit a reef and our cargo escaped.' He tugs the rope, drawing the pony to him. 'With the tide going out we were unable to float off, so we're pumping water and stemming the leak.'

Sario doesn't understand everything, but the white man seems friendly, smiling and yarning. More sailors stride up the beach carrying rope, their dinghy behind them on the shore. 'How many have you caught?' they call.

The thick fog is lifting and Sario can see the carrier ship in the distance, cables and anchors holding it in position on the coral, stopping it toppling and sinking.

His uncles come down the hill, leading more beasts. They hand them over and the sailors swap the twine leads for rope. 'I'll wager this cranky cream stallion caused you some trouble,' the redhead says, tugging its lead. 'We're shipping the mob down from Timor. These ponies do well in the heat and rain; they're hardy beasts and resistant to diseases.' He pats the pony's neck. 'They'll make good packhorses for explorers and graziers.'

Thaati invites the sailors to sit, and gestures to Sario and Esike to lop the tops off coconuts for the men to drink.

A sailor points to a shady beach-almond tree. 'Can we tie the ponies there?'

An elder nods.

'We are very appreciative of your help and sorry about the damage to your gardens,' the sailor continues. 'There will be a reward.'

Sario listens to their yarning, interested. The sailors are loud and blustery, but not pushy and bullying like the white trader or snappy like the white boss at the shelling station. They're different, they show no sign of taking advantage; they came only to collect their ponies.

'We'll float off with the high tide, there's not much damage,' the redhead says, looking out at his ship. 'Can you spare a piece of wood to patch the leak?'

Sario follows his gaze. What is their carrier like? He's seen small cargo-traders when he's walked out at low tide and carried supplies in from the boats, but he's never seen a ship as big as this up close, or met a pale, spotted sailor with hair as red as a coral trout.

It's a happy visit, with lots of yarning and hand signals. Sario listens, fascinated by their white-talk and friendliness. One of the sailors catches a sea-snake in the lagoon and cuts it open, explaining its working to the boys. Esike is impressed. 'Maybe not all white men take advantage,' he says.

Leilani brings out her healing balms and treats a sailor with an ugly sore on his leg. She explains which plants to use for tropical ulcers and how the milky sap of the mangrove plant will relieve the sting of a stonefish, if ever they step on one. She mixes burnt ash into a thicker potion for the cuts on the brown pony's neck. '*Kemu*, plant,' she says, giving the sailor a small stick plant wrapped in banana leaf.

'*Kemu*,' the sailor repeats, and laughs. He asks how they navigate without the help of sea-charts. 'It's a difficult strait,' he says. 'Torres waters fester with coral reefs.'

'Go far to fish. Trade with mainland,' an elder explains, pointing south towards the colonies of Australia and north to New Guinea. 'Long way.'

'You trade with Cape York tribes?' The sailor is surprised to hear the clan travel so far in their small island canoe.

Thaati points to the sky. 'Read stars and wind and clouds.' They know about the currents, the push and pull of the sea.

'Dig *tik*?' Sario suggests. He takes the red-haired sailor down to the shore and shows him how they dig for bait in the wet sand.

The sailor watches for the change of tide. 'It's time to swim the ponies back to the ship,' he says. 'Come and collect your reward.'

Reward? Sario doesn't understand his white-talk.

The redhead smiles. 'A reward is a gift, a thank-you.'

'*Eso*.' Sario smiles.

The elders decide that Sario and Esike will go, in the smaller two-man canoe. Esike grins with excitement, but Sario is not so sure. He wants to see the big boat up close, but a ship full of ghost-white men bothers him.

They follow the sailor's dinghies, a pony swimming either side tugging their small canoe along. He trusts the sailor with the spotty face and big smile, but what about the other white men on the ship? He's given the sailor a turtle-shell hook and told him of his dream to pump-dive, to wear a big helmet and walk the sea-floor.

'Are you a good diver? Would you raise a lot of shell?'

Sario nods.

'Go to Thursday Island,' the man says. 'Pearling skippers want strong young divers. One of them might teach you to pump-dive.'

Sario explains that he doesn't want to leave his island and family, they need him.

The sailor nods. 'But don't let anything keep you from your dream.'

Sario squirms and doesn't reply. How can he tell the man that he's afraid of white men? That his cousins Naku and Kadub went with a white skipper and never came back?

Chapter Seven

Sario peers out at first light. The carrier ship has gone, but he won't forget the kind sailor who gave him the small knife. He strokes the sharp blade and slips it into his woven belt. It isn't long and shiny like the trader's machete, but he will take it everywhere. The sailors gave them many rewards for catching the beasts – biscuits and fruit and coins. 'Valuable cargo, these ponies,' the red-haired sailor said, slapping their rumps to move them on board. The money pieces were flat and round and not useful at all – a strange way to trade. But the elders were thankful for them, passing the coins around and babbling excitedly. '*Eso*, help clan.'

Thaati watches the sky. He's been waiting for the steady weather, the right currents, but it won't last long; the winds will soon be back churning the sea. This will be their last long voyage for some time.

Sario loads the coconuts and balances the weight in the canoe. They'll leave the coconuts on the bird island if they get that far. It's their tradition, to help sea travellers in distress.

Apu calls to Leilani to hurry up, but her voice is growing faint, her breathing a struggle. Leilani doesn't hear her mother and ambles to the canoe, stopping to pick a small yellow flower for her hair.

An elder gestures to Sario to take the bow position again. 'Man's work,' he says, as they push out. The breeze picks up and the boys push the mat sails up the poles and ease back from paddling.

Esike yarns about catching the beasts and visiting the big ship, but Sario's thoughts are on the redhead's advice to follow his dream. Could the clan buy a lugger . . . raise enough shell? He looks around at the old divers, their bodies thin, their faces weary, and shakes his head. It's a foolish dream.

They toss vines and catch fish as they sail on, and pull into a small uninhabited island at sundown. The thin straggly trees are casting shadows on the sand, their leaves drooping with thirst. 'Trees green again soon when rain comes,' Leilani says. She's already clearing and preparing their gardens to plant before the wet-time. She drops off to sleep planning her new crops.

The sun is high in the sky when they spot the bird island with its towering white lighthouse and glass windows glinting in the sun. The keeper's cottages and storage sheds are as small as ants beside it. Seabirds are shrieking and diving and splattering the rock face white with their droppings, and at the far end a huddle of fishing boats bob in the waves. Sario spots a cutter close by swinging on its anchor and sees three men rowing back to it from the island, a large sack of goods in their dinghy.

'Unload coconuts,' Thaati says, when they reach the shallow water on the far side of the island. The clan push their paddles into the sand to hold the canoe steady while Sario gathers up the loose nuts and pushes them into his net. 'We look for reefs and come back,' Thaati says, as they paddle off.

Sario floats the coconuts ashore, his fish net bulging. He can see the gaping mouth of the cave and the skinny tree growing at its entrance. He drags the net up over the rocks, the big nuts bouncing noisily. A large flock of birds rise from the trees, squawking and flapping out of the valley.

He steps into the big gloomy cave and waits for his eyes to adjust. Enough sunlight is streaming in to see the rough dark walls and the strange words and pictures scrawled on them, faint drawings of sailing ships, stick men, fish and turtles. A dark passage at the back disappears into the blackness and who knows where – he'd never go there. He sees the food stores through the dusty haze, the barrels of water and casks of preserved meat, some split open. Empty bottles lie strewn about and biscuit cases broken open. He drags the coconuts across the dirt floor and stacks them next to a tin chest. He lifts the lid, curious.

‘There you are!’

He spins at the white-man voice, fear creeping up his spine. The tall ghost-white trader fills the cave opening. Sario feels for the small knife in the back of his belt.

‘What are you doing, boy?’ The man steps forward, squinting into the darkness.

Sario backs away, the coconuts rolling at his feet.

‘Are you stealing the provisions?’ The man’s deep, bitter laugh echoes through the dimness. ‘You don’t look like a stranded seaman in need of food!’

Sario flattens his body against the cave wall and watches him prowl.

‘How often do you come here? Did your clan make this filthy mess?’ He props up a broken cask. ‘The beef and pork are ruined!’ His voice gets louder and angrier. ‘This cave is a safe haven for shipwrecked sailors, a refuge. Not a place to rob and ransack!’

Sario slides along the wall, his bare feet making no sound in the dust.

‘The big light has made the waters safer to navigate, there are not so many shipwrecks these days.’ The trader reaches into the tin chest and takes out a white bundle. ‘And we don’t see too many letters nowadays.’ He flicks through the papers, distracted.

Sario watches him, puzzled by his yarning. Is he trying to be friendly now?

‘Back then it was a post office, you know. Sea travellers left parcels and letters for passing ships to carry on.

There was a visitor's book and pens and ink and paper, and ship's captains left reports of bad storms and shipping hazards.' He stops and turns suddenly. 'Did your mob destroy those as well?'

Sario is edging towards the opening, his fingernails gouging dirt from the wall. He should have taken more notice of the fishing boats at the far end of the island – he would have seen the trader's lugger, recognised its high cabin and sharp hull. Instead, he was watching the men with the sack in their dinghy. Did they make the mess, wreck the stores and carry food away?

'I saw your canoe leave, boy.' The trader moves closer, his voice menacing. He snatches up a brown bottle and pops the cork. 'You come with me now.'

Sario tightens his grip on the knife.

'You want to earn money don't you, boy? Help your clan?' The trader takes a swig from the bottle, glancing at Sario every now and then as he slides along the wall.

The opening is close now. Sario can see the sea and the rocks and the white man's dinghy. Where is his clan? His canoe?

The trader moves closer. 'There's no place to go, you know.'

Sario can feel the warm sun on his face and smell the fresh salty air. Should he make a run for it?

The trader pounces. 'You're coming with me now.' He slams Sario against the wall. 'You're not wasting any more of my time, boy.'

Sario's head smacks the hard earth. His eyes blur. Dizzy. He draws the knife slowly from his belt.

The trader digs his fingers into Sario's shoulders. 'I hear you're a good strong diver, you raise a lot of shell.' He grins. 'You will be my new boy!'

Sario struggles to get away, the stink of stale tobacco clogging his nose, blocking his throat.

'That was a *yes* I heard, wasn't it?' If the boy agrees to go with him, he'll have no trouble with the law, no backlash from Aboriginal protectors. 'I'll let your father know you're with me.'

Sario slides his knife slowly to his front. He is *not* his boy!

'Let the knife go. Drop it!'

Sario feels his wrist twist and pain burn up his arm – his bones will snap! All feeling goes from his fingers. He drops the knife.

The trader bends to pick it up, and Sario sees movement outside. A large canoe is gliding in behind the ghost man's dinghy. Binghis! Are they friendly? Does he know them?

The trader notices Sario's eyes widen and turns to follow his gaze. 'Binghis!' The mainland mob are coming across the rocks, their spears drawn. He reaches for his pistol.

Sario slips from his grip and runs out of the cave.

A spear stops him. 'Where you go, brudda?' The sharp tip is poking his belly. Arrows are drawn. Spears pointed. Sario raises his hands and studies the circle of painted faces. Does he know them? Does his clan trade with this tribe?

'What do you want?' The trader slots his pistol back in its holster; his gun is no match for their arrows. 'Tobacco? Sugar? Biscuits?'

Sario feels another sharp prod. The boy with the spear is waving him away. He recognises him! Wide smile, all teeth, a deep scar above his lip. They've traded. He and Esike exchanged a turtle-shell hook and pronged fishing spear for the boy's fine bow. It's a good bow, too – it brings down the fat white pigeons.

He feels the spear prod his belly again and sees the boy flick his head. *Go!* Sario runs and leaps off the rocks. He wades out; he can see the canoe in the distance. He swims for his life.

The men drag him into the canoe. Esike is bubbling with news: he's found a large patch of sea-slugs without any help from his clever cousin! '*Gorsar*, plenty!' He spreads his arms wide.

Sario sinks into the canoe, his chest thumping, his mind back at the cave. Esike pokes him with a paddle. '*Maalu!*' Can't Sario see the sea is getting choppy and they have a long way to go? He's raised the sails already, but they'll still need to paddle home.

Sario doesn't move, doesn't accept his paddle.

Esike notices the colour draining from Sario's face, his skin a sickly grey. What is wrong with him? 'You *aka-pali*, frightened?'

Sario nods, reliving his fear . . . the pain burning up his arm, his head slamming against the hard wall. '*Markai*,' he whispers, wondering what will happen next time they meet.

Esike nudges him to tell him more, but Sario is deep in thought. Will the *markai* go away now, or will he make trouble? The elders should ban him from the island, stop all trading with him. But what then? His mind knots with questions. The clan has been trading with him a long time and he's not one to cross. Who else will buy their harvest? The shelling-station boss is a cranky *mabaeg*, difficult to barter with, and the stretch of sea to get there is a dangerous crossing. Is there another trader?

Thaati stops the canoe to dive. The sea is rough, but the divers go down to check the muddy bottom. They could be lucky and find a few pearl-shells.

Sario is on his way up when he spots the dark shape. '*Baidam*, shark!' he yells, as he hits the surface. He tosses his pearl-shell into the canoe and scrambles in, pulling his aunties up and calling to others as they surface. Everyone is in – except Leilani. Didn't she hear him? He sees her swimming out and shouts again. '*Baidam!*' But she disappears underwater.

Sario leaps in, his heart pounding, the shark passing over him. Leilani is on her way up, a pearl-shell in her hand. *Shark!* He points, and they kick up together, thrashing and splashing, the only way they know to scare off a shark. The dark shape swims on, chasing a large fish.

Leilani's eyes glisten with tears as Thaati pulls her into the canoe. She's deaf, she cries – she didn't hear their calls. She drops the shell into the canoe and rubs her ears. 'Ears *kikiri.*' Her pain is bad and she is frightened.

Thaati groans as they sail away, his worries increasing. He spots birds circling and throws out a line. There's little fight in the fish, no tangled lines, no panic; the fish are easily hooked. All the panic is in the canoe.

Chapter Eight

When he's packed the shells in sacks and spread the sea-slugs on racks to dry in the sun, Sario approaches his father on the beach. Thaati is staring out to sea, his face drawn, his shoulders slumped. Is he ready to hear more troubling news? Sario drops onto the sand beside him and tells him about the white man in the cave. 'A wicked *markai*,' he says, describing how the man slammed his head against the wall and demanded he go with him and be his boy. How he twisted his wrist until his arm burned. How the binghis scared the man with their arrows and spears.

Thaati sits listening and brooding, his forehead creasing with worry. The white trader is not going to stop – he wants to take Sario no matter what! Thaati stands suddenly and strides off to discuss it with the elders. Should they send Sario with a man who is so hot-headed? They need the trader to take their harvest, he's the only one who returns regularly, but they haven't seen this violent side of him. Will he make trouble if they refuse to let Sario go? He could make serious accusations to the government and bring the police magistrate to their island. The pearl-shell time is getting closer, the rain clouds building. What should they do?

Sario curls up on the sand. Why is he such a weak scared boy, too frightened to stand up to the man? Too afraid to prove his skills? Why isn't he strong like his warrior ancestors? He should be earning money for his clan, making the trader respect him, yarning confidently like he did with the redhead sailor.

He gets up and wanders the beach, kicking up sand and grappling with his fears. The clan needs him to stand up and be a man, take responsibility. Leilani is lost in her silence and will not dive deep again, and Apu is suffering and short of breath with little air in her lungs to dive or sing. The old people are growing weary and slowing down. What will happen to their small clan, their island paradise? His life is changing. Growing up is hard.

He hears Esike whistle. 'Come, Sario! Dive wreck! *Malil*, metal!' He's pushing their small canoe through the shallows, the water clear and sparkling blue. Sario runs and jumps in. The wreck isn't too far from the island – they've seen the debris floating on their way back from fishing. Will they find anything? Metal anchors and chains and fittings are good to trade.

They paddle to where timber planks are floating and the mast is poking up out of the water. The cutter is lying broken and abandoned on the coral, its anchor chain snapped. They struggle to raise the anchor but it's too heavy, so they lift the chain and attach it to the canoe; they'll try to drag the anchor home. They dive over the wreck, salvaging anything they can: forks and spoons, glass bottles, ropes, fishing cord and hooks. Esike brings up a boathook with a rope attached. A cranky sea-snake whips about his legs and then zigzags off across the top of the water. He dangles the hook over a clam on the sea floor, its large shell open for prey; sensing movement, it closes quickly and locks the boathook in. They raise the heavy clam on the hook, heaving and dragging it into the canoe. '*Gorsar*.' There's plenty of meat to share.

They've heard many stories of sunken ships and silver coins buried on islands. 'Wish we know where treasure be,' Sario says. White-man's money would solve all his problems. 'Buy tools. Buy lugger. Pump-dive.' He laughs at his foolish dream as he goes back down with Esike's small knife to slash the sails from the masts.

He gathers the wet, heavy canvas into the canoe and looks around. Where are the cutter's crew and passengers? He scans the small sand cays nearby. Has a skipper been and picked them up? Surely they've all been rescued – the Strait is a busy shipping channel. He sees a large carrier in the distance, its white sails billowing, and behind it a steamer puffing smoke from its funnels. A small cargo vessel is crossing their path, delivering goods to islands. Sario squints into the sun at an approaching boat – a pearling lugger. He scans its sleek lines and high cabin and scrambles into the canoe. '*Markai*,' he yells down to Esike, splashing the water, hurrying him to come up and start paddling.

Their small canoe will barely move, no matter how hard they pull on their paddles – the anchor from the wreck is holding it fast. Sario tries to unhook the chain, but he's useless, his fingers twitching with nerves.

Esike shoves him aside. '*Uzari*, go.' He'll do it! The trader's lugger is closing in.

'How was your fishing, boys?' the trader shouts. 'Did you harvest plenty of slugs? Raise lots of shell?'

Esike keeps fiddling with the heavy chain and Sario tries to help, but his fingers tremble. How will they escape him? Their small canoe is no match for the trader's lugger. Sario reaches for his fishing spear and grips it tight. What will the *markai* do? Run them down? Swim across and drag him away?

'That boy is a strong young diver,' the trader says to his crewmate. 'He'll be one of my swimming-divers this season.' He hesitates. 'Trouble is, darkies don't give up their boys without a fight, and I'm not sure he'll stay. You can't trust them, you know. Before the missionaries came, they'd sink a spear in your back and take your scalp.'

Water swirls around the wreck. The strong current tugs at the chain and it finally unhooks. Sario and Esike paddle for their lives.

'I'll be back to trade your catch of bêche-de-mer when it's smoked and bagged,' the trader calls. 'Are you ready to dive, boy? Make money?' He'll bide his time and wait a little longer. The clan will cooperate and hand over the boy – every Islander wants something.

Sario paddles as fast as he can, his mind racing. How does the trader know about Esike's large catch of slugs?

The lugger turns and comes towards them; they're in the deep water right in its path. What's the white man doing? The lugger swerves suddenly and veers away, the small canoe rocking violently in its wake, its mat sails flapping. The boys struggle to keep it upright. What should they do? Toss out the metal and lighten the load? Abandon the canoe and swim for their island? It's a long way back. They see the trader reaching for something. Is it his pistol? Is he going to shoot at them and sink their canoe? They hear him yell and see something flying towards them. 'A gift for you, boy!'

They duck as it lands in the canoe with a thud. What is it? They can't see, it's fallen behind the wet canvas sails. Sario quickens his paddling, fear weighing like an anchor in his gut. He sees the lugger peel away and wonders . . . is it his small knife he dropped in the cave?

It's a small, heavy tin. When they reach the island, Sario pierces the top and watches the thick white treacle ooze out. Leilani scoops a little with her finger and puts it to her tongue. '*Upiri*?' he asks. Maybe the white man is trying to poison him, make him sick.

'Mmm, *mital*, sweet.' She licks her lips and trickles the delicious creamy condensed milk onto her warm damper. '*Nutai*, try,' she offers.

Sario shakes his head and storms off to the rocks. The trader has taken his knife and given him this sweet milk in exchange. He's not eating it! Nothing could rid him of the man's sour taste. He picks up small oyster-covered rocks and hurls them into the fire in frustration. He'll eat oysters instead!

He sees a cargo boat arrive and drop anchor well off shore. It calls occasionally, full of interesting things. The clan wade out excitedly with coconuts and fish, hoping to exchange them for flour and kerosene. 'I have nails and wire and candles,' the captain says, encouraging them to buy. He points out items the aunties might like. 'Calico? Beads? Fancy soaps?'

Thaati picks up a metal spade and axe.

'I want cash for those, they're quality tools,' the captain says. 'No masks or bamboo spears.'

Thaati puts the tools down and offers the captain a pumpkin and paw-paw in exchange for a little medicine for his sick wife. He taps his chest and coughs, indicating that her lungs are weak, her breathing difficult.

Leilani carries the small bottle of elixir back to her mother and squeezes noni fruit for Apu to drink with her medicine. She rolls out a sleeping mat and massages Apu with oil. She continues making her mother a comfortable pillow, breaking open the last of the pods she gathered from the kapok tree and pulling out the fluffy cream fibre. She puts the fluff in a basket and stirs it with a stick to make the seeds fall to the bottom, shaking the basket as she goes. She stuffs the soft fibre into the clean flour-sack and stitches the top closed with vine. It takes a while, but Leilani's happy with the pillow. 'Lift *kuik*,' she says, slipping the fluffy new pillow gently under Apu's head.

'*Eso*.' Apu whispers, thanking her for the new pillow, so soft and comfortable.

When he's back from fishing Sario sits with his mother on the mat under the shady almond tree. He'll carve her something special from the driftwood he's found on the beach. Apu is so thin and frail, he hopes a turtle will cheer her up.

He rounds the small head and marks where the big eyes will go. After they've eaten and the fire is dying, he holds his carving up to show her.

'*Eso*.' Apu nods and smiles, proud of her son. 'Good carver. Good diver, Sario.'

Over many sunrises the carving progresses as Sario sits comforting his mother. He is shaping the turtle's wide flippers when he sees the pearling lugger arrive. He stiffens, his gaze taking in the sleek hull, the high cabin.

Should he run now . . . or wait to see if the trader has brought back his small knife?

The ghost man strides up the beach, tucking in his long white shirt. He lifts his wide-brimmed hat and greets the elders, the uncles and aunties. 'You need rice? Oats? Sugar?' His sack bulges with goods. 'I have jam and molasses and fancy enamel bowls. I'll take all your bêche-de-mer and shell. What else do you have? Yams? Bananas?'

Sario stays on the mat with Apu, watching the *markai* lay out his goods, waiting to see if his small knife appears. He's ready to slip away when he needs to, where the ghost man won't find him!

The trader takes out the long shiny machete and places it on the yarning log. He glances about until he spots the boy under a tree with his mother. 'You want the machete?' he calls. 'I need you in my crew. The dive season is starting soon.'

Sario wants to shout back, *Where is my knife? Where are my cousins Kadub and Naku?* But Thaati is pleading with the trader to exchange the shells for cash – he needs to buy more medicine from the cargo boats. 'Take beautiful turtle-shell. Give white-man's money. Please.'

The trader nods. 'I'll do you a deal,' he says, handing Thaati a gift. 'I'll pay you cash. I'll take all your turtle-shell . . . and your boy.'

Thaati accepts the gift, a small plant with green shoots. 'It's a tamarind tree,' the trader says. 'The fruit has a bittersweet taste.' He passes Leilani a length of cloth. 'Here's a gift for you, girlie. Sew yourself a pretty dress.'

He's bribing them! He's trying to win the clan over with a plant and cloth and sweet milk! Can't they see it? Sario drops his wood carving on the mat and slips away. He creeps behind the huts and up past the spring where an auntie is bathing, past the green patch of grass and along the well-worn track to the gardens and into the hills beyond. He drags branches and makes a lean-to under a tree, high in the hills where no one will come looking. He can see the lugger clearly from here, he'll know when the trader leaves.

He hears his uncle moving through the dry bush below, calling his name. Sario prickles with guilt as he curls up to think, uncertain now if hiding away is the right thing. No one disobeys his elders. What will his wise uncle say? That he's a scared boy not ready to do a man's job? That he runs away from his responsibilities? The white trader says he wants strong divers. Maybe the *markai* won't hurt him if he proves his skill in raising shell. The man needs him in his crew!

Sario knocks down the branches and stands and stretches. The sky is darkening, the birds quiet; an eerie silence hangs over the island. He sees the lugger leaving. Next time he'll go with the trader. He'll demand his respect. He'll help his clan. He collects sticks for the fire as he makes his way back down the hill, his mind made up.

In the glow of the fire on the beach, he sees the dark shapes of his clan gathering under the almond tree. Is something wrong with Apu? Sario drops the sticks and runs.

She's gasping for breath and pressing her chest. 'Medicine,' she whispers. Sario looks around for his father. Where is Thaati?

Leilani steps forward with a small medicine bottle, uncorks it and holds it up to the firelight. There's not much elixir left – Sario sees the dark line at the bottom. '*Markai*,' Leilani says, rolling her eyes towards the sea.

Sario knows the white man has gone and that the medicine bottle is almost empty, but can't she make more? He signals to her in the firelight. *Do something! Mix a plant potion!*

She waves her hand to the sea, tears glistening on her lashes. 'Thaati gone.'

Gone? Gone where? What does she mean? 'Thaati's gone with the white trader?'

Leilani nods, placing her hands together as if she's diving.

Sario slumps on the mat beside Apu. His father has taken his place, he's gone diving with the white man? He looks at his wise uncle. Is it true?

His uncle nods. 'The trader want you, Sario. I look for you, call you. The *markai* will not leave without a diver, so your thaati has to go. Esike too young, other divers too old.'

Sario's eyes well with tears. He was hiding away . . . and now it's too late.

'Your thaati not want to leave your sick mother,' his uncle continues, 'but the white man is angry. *You dishonour our deal, you disobey rules. I report you to the government.*'

Sario shudders. What if Thaati doesn't come back? What if he disappears like Kadub and Naku?

'No medicine worth white-man trouble,' Apu whispers. 'Thaati will dive and bring money home.'

'We be alright,' his uncle says, as they carry Apu to the hut to sleep. 'Your thaati's pay will buy medicine.'

Sario's belly squirms like a drum full of eels. He was too scared to help his clan, and now Thaati has gone.

'The trader has his diver now, he leave us be,' his uncle adds. 'Not all white men so forceful – remember the kind sailors who came for the ponies and gave you a knife.'

He doesn't have the knife now! Or his thaati! All he has is problems.

Leilani sweeps the floor mats with a stiff palm-leaf broom and rolls out a new sleeping mat for Apu. She rubs her mother down with coconut oil, filling the night air with its fresh woody smell. She slides the soft kapok pillow under her head and hands Sario the empty medicine bottle – Apu is his responsibility now.

Chapter Nine

Sario paces the sand, begging the elders to help him. He did the wrong thing and he's sorry, but Apu is much worse, she's struggling for every breath and fretting for Thaati. What can he do? He's tried to settle her, squeezing fruit to ease her sore throat and giving her the last drops of medicine. Leilani is crushing plants and making more *lukup* and his aunties are preparing steam inhalants and clearing her lungs. Everyone is praying along with her for Thaati's safe return, but when will that be? 'Apu is fading away.'

'We'll take her to Waiben, to the white-man's doctor,' the elders announce after yarning around the fire.

At sun-up they push the big canoe out, their eyes on the sky and their hearts pounding with worry; the seas are choppy and their pretty turquoise bay is turning dark and menacing. It will be a long crossing.

The strongest men paddle out, but the winds are increasing and the sea swelling. Rolling waves push them back and swamp the canoe. The boys bail water quickly, scooping it up in big bailer shells, but the surf is relentless.

Sario helps carry Apu back up the beach to the safety of the hut; sand whipped up by the wind is blasting his skinny body and stinging him all over. His thin calico wrap blows open; knotted at his waist, it offers little protection.

Three sunrises pass and Apu is growing weaker, but not the wind. Wild seas roll in, crashing and thundering on the rocks, shooting tall streaks of white foam into the sky. Sario paces the small hut, listening to his mother wheezing. His father taught him to fix a leak in the canoe, and to weave a new leaf into a sail to mend a hole . . . but how can he fix Apu if he can't get her off the island? Thaati should be here making decisions, and he, Sario, should be diving for the white man, not hiding away like a slug with no backbone. He should be the one earning money and helping his clan, standing up to the white trader and demanding respect. His father is probably pump-diving by now!

Leilani rubs Apu down with oil, massaging it through her hair and over her frail body. 'Apu is skin and bone,' she cries. What can she do?

Sario escapes to the palm trees. What can he say? He doesn't have the answer. The long green leaves thrash in the wind and heavy nuts thud to the ground, but the wind has dropped a little, the wild surf is easing back.

They'll know by sun-up if they can leave for Waiben. He picks up a strip of coconut husk and cleans his teeth, rubbing the stiff fibre across his teeth and over his gums, feeling the smoothness with his tongue.

He spots a ship a long way out and hears Esike call. Can they flag it down, attract the skipper's attention? Sario runs to the shore, waving frantically. Esike jumps up and down, shouting and waving his arms, but the ship goes on, tossing in the waves, far away.

It's later, when they're picking up the falling palm leaves and dragging them to the fire that they spot the steamship coming from Badu, much closer to them and heading south. 'Steamer! Waiben!' Sario shouts, whipping off his calico wrap and waving desperately to attract the skipper's attention. He tilts the empty condensed milk tin to reflect the sun's rays – back and forth, back and forth. Esike runs and gets the small mirror he's found washed up on the beach, and shouts to his younger cousins to join him. They're a noisy mob, shouting and jumping and begging. *Please will somebody see them?*

The steamer veers suddenly towards them. 'They're coming!' Sario shouts and runs, hollering to everyone to help carry Apu to the beach. He signals to Leilani to bring their belongings, their sleeping mats and cooking pots. Who knows how long they'll be away?

He watches the crew drop anchor and lower a dinghy, and yarns excitedly with his wise uncle. His uncle's eyesight is failing, but he can see the dinghy! 'Men are coming. Take

Apu white-man doctor,' Sario says as the dinghy progresses slowly towards them through the choppy waves, two men pulling hard on the oars. He'll take responsibility. He'll stand up and do a man's job!

The men jump out. 'What's wrong? Do you have an emergency here?'

'Help Apu!' Sario begs, pointing to his mother lying on a mat in her loose cotton dress. He lowers his eyes in respect, as is custom, but all white men look the same to him – except for the red-headed sailor.

One man crouches and puts his ear to Apu's wheezing chest. He asks her to cough and places his hand on her forehead. 'She's hot with fever,' he says. 'It's a long way to Thursday Island and the seas are rough, I'm not sure she will make it. Who knows when we'll arrive?' He sees the desperate looks on their faces and consults the elders.

The men are troubled and yarning; it's not right for the man to be touching a female. What should they do? He's friendly-touching, trying to help, but it's disrespectful – not custom.

Sario can't hear their yarning, but he sees the elders are fidgety and uncertain. He places the palms of his hands together and prays like the missionaries taught him.

'Thursday Island does have a medical practitioner,' the crewman says, then pauses. He's unsure if the doctor would treat an Islander woman, though he's heard reports that the doctor has never failed any patient in their time of sickness. 'Hurry up,' he decides. 'Get her in the dinghy.'

The elders nod, agreeing that the steamship is her only hope, and that Sario and Leilani will go with her. They lift Apu gently into the dinghy and load in the baskets, the pots and pans and sleeping mats, and a kerosene drum filled with food from the garden.

The crewman watches. 'You can't live on Thursday Island, you know. You can't stay there permanently. No Islanders are allowed to settle.'

Sario shakes his head. 'No stay.' Apu will get the white-doctor medicine and they'll return home; it shouldn't take long. He steps into the dinghy after Leilani and waves to his clan. He looks at his ill mother as they row to the ship, tears trickling down his cheeks. He remembers the lessons she's taught him since he was a small boy . . .

A good hunter waits absolutely still; his barb is sharp, his spear balanced. He angles his body and spears down hard. A good hunter gets his fish.

But a woman fishes the easy way. She carries her basket down to the sea when the tide is going out. She puts it in the waves and holds it there with a stick. Then she sits back and watches the basket fill with fish – plenty for everyone!

Chapter Ten

The big steamer is swinging on its anchor chain. 'Ships are travelling in convoy because of the dangerous seas,' the crewman says, as they clamber aboard. Sario looks back at his island, his eyes wet with tears. He should be excited to be on the big steamship, but he's panicky and sick inside. He's leaving his clan, his beautiful island, going who knows where! He's on his own, responsible for his sick mother and deaf sister . . . and no thaati or uncles to help him! He rushes to the railing and heaves his guts over the side.

Leilani cries; she's scared too. How will they find their way around the big new island? How will they find the white-man doctor? How will he fix Apu?

Sario feels for the money in his calico wrap, the round flat coins he's tied in a knot. The elders gave him every coin they had. Are the bigger coins worth more than the small ones? Does he give them all to the doctor? Will he need to work and earn more?

'Waiben is big island – plenty divers?' he asks the crewman.

The man sees the knot of coins and understands the boy's concern. 'You should get work, cleaning and painting. The fishing luggers are laid up for repairs.'

Huge waves slam into the steamer and push the ship off course. 'Sea conditions are treacherous,' the crewman says, looking around, checking for other crew. One man is up the mast keeping a lookout for rocks and reefs. Another is continually raising and lowering a rope over the side. 'The lead weight hits the bottom and gives us the depth,' the crewman explains. 'See the coloured tags on the rope – they indicate the fathoms, the depth of the water. Torres Strait is strewn with hazards.' He shades his eyes and looks up ahead. 'Look – that vessel's run aground, she's stuck hard and fast on the sandbank.'

In the distance, men are scaling the masts and taking down sails, putting out anchors and steadying the ship. Small boats of crewmen are being lowered to inspect the damage. Sario's steamer alters course towards the leaning ship.

'That was a narrow escape!' a portly captain calls up from his dinghy. 'The breeze was freshening and the ship was going fast to the rocks. We heaved goods overboard to lighten the load and fortunately this sandbank saved us.' He waves them off. 'Thank you for your willingness to assist. We'll stay with the ship, pump the water and mend the leaks, and wait for the winds to ease.'

The crewman encourages Sario to talk as they sail on. 'You're a shy boy,' he says. 'What will you do while your mother has treatment?'

Sario looks down at his toes. Do all white men yarn this way? Ask questions? The man's confronting, like the trader and the sailors, asking him personal things – his business.

'Are you a good diver?'

Sario curls his toes at the man's blunt questioning, then nods – the crewman could be helpful.

'You'll get work on the dive boats – the pearl-shell season is starting soon. But you'll have to make arrangements for your mother and sister. Pearling luggers stay at sea for months at a time, they only come in to unload their catch and restock supplies.'

Sario tightens his grip on the ship's railing and stares ahead. How could he leave Apu and Leilani in a strange place? How could he stay on a boat with a white man? Could his mother's treatment take that long? He watches the small islands and sand cays as the ship steams past. Some are empty and desolate, others have cooking fires burning on the beach and canoes laid up in the mangroves. What would Thaati do?

'Go to the dry dock if you're wanting work now. Skippers are cleaning and repairing their vessels before the pearl-shell season starts.'

Sario sees the hills are black on one island, where a cooking fire has gotten out of control and burnt the trees and dry scrubland. The smaller islands are not inhabited, but along their high water marks, coconut palms are growing.

'Captains plant palms on small islands to help them navigate,' the crewman says. 'Tall coconuts stand out, making the islands more visible.' He smiles as Leilani approaches them shyly. 'And if a ship strikes the coral, the coconuts will provide food for the passengers and crew.'

Sario gazes at the coconut trees and blinks back tears. If he were home now, he'd be gathering and husking coconuts. He'd be lighting a fire and roasting his catch. His aunties would be singing and making damper and boiling fish-heads for soup. Esike would be combing the shore with his small cousins and dragging home washed-up treasures.

The crewman realises the girl is looking for food for her mother, and leads them to the galley. 'Come and have supper.'

The *kai kai* looks different. There's nothing like *sop sop* on banana leaves; it's mutton and beans served on white china plates! Leilani scrunches her face and scoops a little soup from a pot into a pannikin for Apu. Sario takes a slice of damper and returns to the deck with the crewman. They watch as men lower the anchors.

'This is a safe anchorage, behind the island and out of the wind,' the crewman says. 'We don't want to drift onto coral in the dark.'

The stars of Tagai are twinkling in the night sky as Sario and Leilani settle their mother on the deck.

The mighty warrior will soon be guiding them home, Leilani whispers to Apu. '*Markai* doctor *gabun-mai*.'

Sario worries. The white healer is Apu's only hope . . . but can they trust him?

Chapter Eleven

The sun's high in the sky as the ship steams into Waiben. Sario and Leilani stare out from the railing; they can hardly believe their eyes. Boats of every size are rocking in the harbour: large schooners tugging at anchor chains, small cutters swinging on ropes, a dirty black hulk loading coal onto a steamship.

As the crew fasten the steamer to the long jetty, the crewman hurries them to the hospital. Apu is weak and fading – there is no time to waste.

It's a long way to the cottage hospital, and everything's so new and different. Sario is tense with nerves. The crewman helps Sario carry Apu, and Leilani follows with another man who helps her with their baskets and belongings. Finally they're walking up the long path and across a veranda with hard wooden floors and glass windows.

Sario clutches his throat as he goes through the doors – strange bitter smells are blocking his nostrils and hurting his throat. He looks at his sister and mother; they're both gagging and choking, their eyes watering. The crewman slaps him on the back. 'All hospitals smell like this, it's the carbolic antiseptic. You'll get used to it.'

Sario struggles with his white-talk, telling the man in the white coat how his mother is suffering 'cold-sick, chest problems'. Leilani explains to the doctor which plant medicines she's given Apu, the ones her aunties taught her to make for healing. '*Sasa* for her cough and *sapur*, flying-fox, to help her breathing.'

A tall white woman directs Apu to a high bed on the hospital veranda. She opens a cabinet and takes out a long metal instrument. Sario tightens his fingers around the cold iron bedhead. What is it? What will they do to Apu? The doctor takes the instrument and nods at them to leave. 'Your mother is in safe hands.' He points to a round clock on the wall and tells them the hospital visiting times. They don't understand.

'Find yourself some temporary accommodation,' the tall woman says, straightening her white veil headdress. 'No Islanders are allowed to live on Thursday Island permanently – it's an administration centre. You could get some work at the dry dock, the fishing boats are laid up there for maintenance.'

Sario looks at Apu lying thin as a stick on the big white hospital bed, her breathing weak, her skin dry and waxy. He doesn't want to leave her in this strange place with its bad smells, but he has no choice. They bow their heads and pray for their mother, tears sliding down their cheeks.

'Come on, we'll find you a place to stay.' The crewman picks up the drum of fruit and vegetables and heads to the door. 'Standing around and weeping won't help.'

An old *mabaeg* sweeping the churchyard tells them there's a hostel at the back for people from the outer islands, where they could stay awhile if they've come to see the doctor or on church business. He rings the church bell on Sundays, he says. Children are spinning tops and kicking balls made of coconut. The crewman steers Sario and Leilani away from the noisy churchyard; he knows of another place. 'It's a small, deserted beach shack,' he says. 'Your mother will need a quieter place to recover away from this hostel – you could be here for a long stay.'

Sario hears a loud *boom*. He drops his basket and covers his ears, cowering. What is it? He stares up at his sister, his eyes wide with fear. Leilani looks at him, puzzled; she hasn't heard a sound. The crewman laughs. 'That's the big gun at the military barracks on Green Hill. The soldiers fire it every day at one o'clock – it's a time signal for the port.'

Sario is still trembling as the crewman leads them down a sandy track. 'It's just an old fishing shack, but you'll be able to shelter here as long as you need. Follow this track back to the hospital.' He drops the drum of food by the doorway and lifts his hat to Leilani as he leaves.

Sario picks up a bucket to fetch water and signs to Leilani as he leaves the shack. He follows the directions the crewman has given him to the well, along a wide dirt track where everything is new and different. White-man's cottages with windows of glass and closing doors sweep up the hillside – nothing like the airy open huts on his island. He passes a wooden building with a wide veranda and bad smells, and men drinking outside. Then a musty-smelling trading store, gloomy inside, with shelves of tins and jars and sacks of yams.

He collects water and firewood and follows the beach track back to the shack. The tide is low and there's a chop in the sea, but he sees fish in the lagoon and hurries to get his spear.

Leilani is outside, cutting the tops off taro. 'Plant garden, big rain coming,' she says, poking the tops in the ground and making small mounds with the soil.

'*Uzari*, go,' he signals back. They'll be home before the taro grows! They'll be gone from this white-man's shack with its iron roof drawing in heat.

'Plant now,' she argues. 'It's time. *Waru* are mating. Big wet coming.'

Noisy children are playing in an upturned dinghy, but Leilani doesn't hear them. Sario grabs his spear and hurries back to the lagoon. He sees other children along the road and men of every skin colour – Japanese fishermen mending sails, Indians tossing bait nets, Chinamen jogging with drums of water on bamboo poles.

The sun goes down and the village falls into darkness as he heads home to cook the fish. Lamps are flickering in hillside houses and a sliver of moonlight casts enough light to find a track back to their beach shack with its leaning timber frame and wooden slats. Where are the beautiful woven-mat walls and a palm-leaf roof to usher in cool sea breezes like his hut at home?

When he's eaten his fish, Sario collapses onto his sleeping mat, his worries weighing heavy on his mind. He's lost Thaati and left his clan, he has to take care of Leilani and his poor frail mother is suffering. Will she recover quickly? Or will he have to work and earn money to pay for her medicine?

He tosses and turns; the white-man's shack is stifling inside, and the hot winds of change keep him stirring.

Chapter Twelve

Sario wakes to the high-pitched *zzz* of a mosquito and grabs his spear. He leaves the shack as dawn is breaking and tramples through dry grass to a new fishing spot. He looks about for turtle tracks in the sand, thinking of the fun he's had with Esike digging up eggs, but there are no drag marks here, no sign of turtles on this island. He hears the jarring bark of an animal and finds a skinny brown dog scuttling crabs on the sand. Close by there's a small fish. Sario spears down hard and carries the fish home on the end of his spear.

Leilani has been to the hospital and back. 'Apu a little better,' she says, smiling. She slips a pretty pink flower in her hair, more confident now finding her way about the big island. Sario beams at the news as he cooks the fish. He'll find a friendly boat skipper to take them home!

He climbs Green Hill and looks for the soldiers the crewman yarned about. They're filing out of their timber military barracks towards the parade ground, and he watches as they wheel the gun carriage into position. *The big gun booms every day at one o'clock*, the crewman said. Sario notices steps leading down to an underground fort behind the wire fence, and shivers when he sees a massive cannon facing out to sea – it's scary but thrilling.

The sea is calming and the water clearing as he walks along the foreshore to the dry dock where boats are laid up. Island boys are arriving in canoes with fish to sell. No, they don't know of any boats going his way, but one gives him a small curved shell and tells him to crack it open. The peanut is hard, nothing like a coconut; it's different from anything Sario has ever seen, like everything else on this island.

A white man pushes a metal tool into his hand. 'Get to work, boy!' he says, shoving him towards a dirty boat, its paint worn off. 'Scrape the barnacles off the hull and clean off all that stinking seaweed.' Sario stumbles and falls, his legs shaking like jellyfish with shock and embarrassment as faces turn and stare. 'Get up! Earn your pay! At the end of the week when the timbers have dried out, you can repair the damage and paint the hull.'

Sario wants to shout back and demand respect, but he shuts his mouth like a clam, picks up the scraping tool and gets to his feet. The man strides off, but his sour smell stays in the air. Sario is sure they'll be gone by the end of the week – Apu is getting better already, isn't she? He feels shame standing there holding the scraping tool, but boys are smiling at him, welcoming him. He turns and starts work.

He soaks up the strange accents as he scrubs the smelly muck off the hull. The boys sing songs from their villages, tunes that remind him of his beautiful island, of Esike and his cousins, his uncles and aunts. He likes the boys' yarning, and laughs at their jokes; their fun breaks up the long day. But Sario notices they're like him, always watching out for the white man. They'll only play when the boss is away, if they want their pay.

Sario listens to the boys yarning about money. 'Half your pay goes into a savings bank, the government keeps it for tax and for your shelter,' a Kanaka boy explains. 'Some of your pay is in food rations and clothes, but you'll get a little pocket money to take home.'

Sario gets more confused as the boy yarns on. What is a savings bank? What is pocket money? And how can he take it home? His calico wrap doesn't have a pocket!

The work is dirty and the day is long, scrubbing and repairing fishing luggers in the hot sun, but he's earning money and the white-man's cash will help pay for Apu's medicine.

The boys yarn about their next jobs in the packing shed. 'You'll get work in the shed once the skippers bring in their catches,' a boy tells Sario.

He shakes his head. 'Go home soon.' He hopes he won't need the shed work now his mother's breathing is getting better; he'll be taking Apu home to recover completely with her kin. She is aching to see her island, as he is, homesick for family and familiarity, the elders yarning, his aunties laughing and singing.

The boys yarn about pump-diving, about the big breathing helmets and lead boots that divers wear, and how they dive the scary Darnley Deeps. 'Japees harvest the most pearl-shell,' one boy says. 'White skippers like Japees. They pay them more money when they dive the Deeps.'

'You good diver?' a boy asks. He's heard rumours that a white man is looking for Sario, a pearling skipper with a sleek lugger.

Sario shudders; he doesn't want to see the *markai* ever again, but he'll have to go and take Thaati's place. He needs Thaati to come and bring money for the bills and help Apu get better.

He drags himself home at the end of the day, dirty and exhausted. The sun is sinking behind the islands, the clouds building, but he still has to fetch water and spear a fish. He throws a stone at a flying-fox and brings it down. He'll pluck it and gut it and roast it on a fire, he'll pull off its black leathery skin and leave the white flesh to eat. He breathes in the sweet smell of frangipani flowers – he'll gather some for Apu before they leave Waiben.

Leilani is sitting under a tree weaving a new sleeping mat before all the daylight disappears. He watches her splitting pandanus leaves into long strips and folding them neatly, over and under, making a pattern of small neat squares. She's found new plants and been mixing

different healing balms, she tells him. Her aunt proud. But the news from the doctor isn't good strong enough to leave,' she says. They'll be Waiben a lot longer.

'How long?' Sario's heart thumps in his c will they manage? The boys say boat work him more than a few shillings a month, and will go to the government store for food – flo and candles. He's been working hard all day the stinking hull and scraping off seaweed an barnacles. Will he be paid any money?

Part Two
~1899~

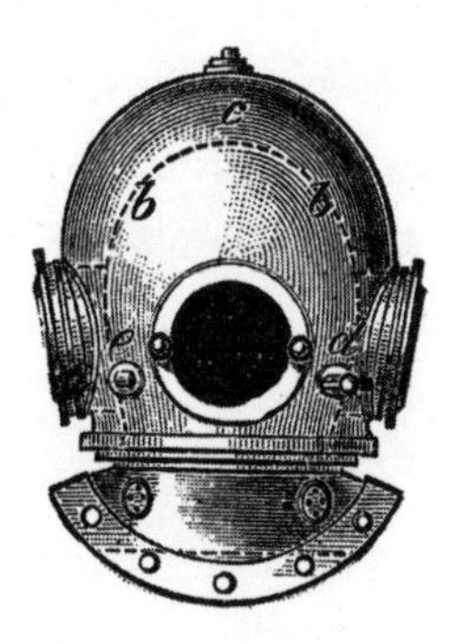

Chapter Thirteen

The dirty, hard work at the dock is over, and the pearling boats are out at sea. Everyone is watching for their return, waiting to see their catches, hoping to earn money.

Sario's chores at the shack are much the same as on his island, fetching water, digging gardens, scraping coconuts and fishing, but he's homesick and misses his thaati and uncles. There's no one here to help him dig a ground-oven, or teach him to read the tides, or warn him to look out for stonefish or the stingray's dangerous tail. But he's finding his way around the big island and learning white-talk listening to the boys.

Leilani picks a flower for her mother's hair as they hurry to the hospital. They're going to bring Apu home to the shack – she's much better, Leilani explains. 'White man's *lukup* is working.'

Apu is out of bed and shuffling about the ward, but still she looks frail, her face gaunt and her body hunched.

'Diving deep for years has damaged your mother's lungs,' the doctor says. 'Take her with you, but don't leave Thursday Island.' He hands Leilani a small bottle of medicine and takes the last of Sario's coins. 'I'll need to observe her regularly and check her breathing over a longer period, and she will need further treatment. Bring her back every few days.'

The tall woman hands Sario another bill as they help Apu to the door. He's paid some bills. Now there's more! His head pounds with worry – there's no money left and Thaati hasn't come. How will he pay for more treatment?

The harbour is rocking with boats, and fishy smells are attracting squawking, hungry gulls as Sario makes his way out along the jetty to the packing shed. The first luggers are back and their catches unloaded.

He peers through the huge open doors and can't believe his eyes. Heaps of crusty pearl-shells as big as hospital plates are slipping and clattering onto the packing shed floor.

'It's a mighty start to the season!' a skipper shouts. Sario sighs with relief; his worries unwinding. He'll get dive work, he'll earn money. He'll learn to pump-dive, for certain! But he needs cash now – Apu can't wait for her medicine. Can he work here today? Scrub shells? Pack crates? He looks around for the boss man. No white faces anywhere.

but boys are smiling at him, welcoming him. He turns and starts work.

He soaks up the strange accents as he scrubs the smelly muck off the hull. The boys sing songs from their villages, tunes that remind him of his beautiful island, of Esike and his cousins, his uncles and aunts. He likes the boys' yarning, and laughs at their jokes; their fun breaks up the long day. But Sario notices they're like him, always watching out for the white man. They'll only play when the boss is away, if they want their pay.

Sario listens to the boys yarning about money. 'Half your pay goes into a savings bank, the government keeps it for tax and for your shelter,' a Kanaka boy explains. 'Some of your pay is in food rations and clothes, but you'll get a little pocket money to take home.'

Sario gets more confused as the boy yarns on. What is a savings bank? What is pocket money? And how can he take it home? His calico wrap doesn't have a pocket!

The work is dirty and the day is long, scrubbing and repairing fishing luggers in the hot sun, but he's earning money and the white-man's cash will help pay for Apu's medicine.

The boys yarn about their next jobs in the packing shed. 'You'll get work in the shed once the skippers bring in their catches,' a boy tells Sario.

He shakes his head. 'Go home soon.' He hopes he won't need the shed work now his mother's breathing is getting better; he'll be taking Apu home to recover completely with her kin. She is aching to see her island, as he is, homesick for family and familiarity, the elders yarning, his aunties laughing and singing.

The boys yarn about pump-diving, about the big breathing helmets and lead boots that divers wear, and how they dive the scary Darnley Deeps. 'Japees harvest the most pearl-shell,' one boy says. 'White skippers like Japees. They pay them more money when they dive the Deeps.'

'You good diver?' a boy asks. He's heard rumours that a white man is looking for Sario, a pearling skipper with a sleek lugger.

Sario shudders; he doesn't want to see the *markai* ever again, but he'll have to go and take Thaati's place. He needs Thaati to come and bring money for the bills and help Apu get better.

He drags himself home at the end of the day, dirty and exhausted. The sun is sinking behind the islands, the clouds building, but he still has to fetch water and spear a fish. He throws a stone at a flying-fox and brings it down. He'll pluck it and gut it and roast it on a fire, he'll pull off its black leathery skin and leave the white flesh to eat. He breathes in the sweet smell of frangipani flowers – he'll gather some for Apu before they leave Waiben.

Leilani is sitting under a tree weaving a new sleeping mat before all the daylight disappears. He watches her splitting pandanus leaves into long strips and folding them neatly, over and under, making a pattern of small neat squares. She's found new plants and been mixing different healing balms, she tells him. Her aunties will be proud. But the news from the doctor isn't good: 'Apu not strong enough to leave,' she says. They'll be staying on Waiben a lot longer.

'How long?' Sario's heart thumps in his chest. How will they manage? The boys say boat work won't pay him more than a few shillings a month, and most of it will go to the government store for food – flour and tea and candles. He's been working hard all day scrubbing the stinking hull and scraping off seaweed and stubborn barnacles. Will he be paid any money?

Part Two
1899

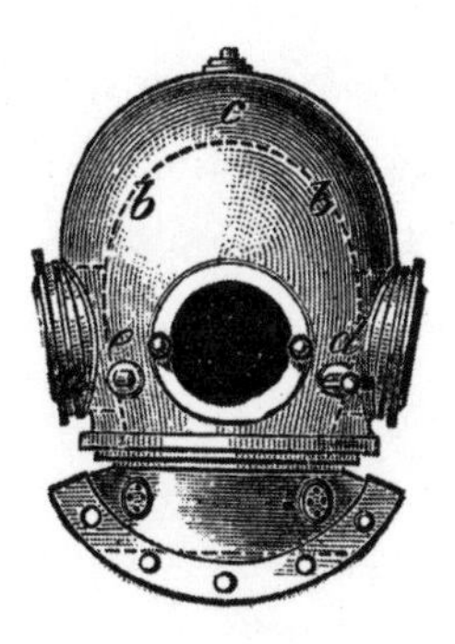

Chapter Thirteen

The dirty, hard work at the dock is over, and the pearling boats are out at sea. Everyone is watching for their return, waiting to see their catches, hoping to earn money.

Sario's chores at the shack are much the same as on his island, fetching water, digging gardens, scraping coconuts and fishing, but he's homesick and misses his thaati and uncles. There's no one here to help him dig a ground-oven, or teach him to read the tides, or warn him to look out for stonefish or the stingray's dangerous tail. But he's finding his way around the big island and learning white-talk listening to the boys.

Leilani picks a flower for her mother's hair as they hurry to the hospital. They're going to bring Apu home to the shack – she's much better, Leilani explains. 'White man's *lukup* is working.'

Apu is out of bed and shuffling about the ward, but still she looks frail, her face gaunt and her body hunched.

'Diving deep for years has damaged your mother's lungs,' the doctor says. 'Take her with you, but don't leave Thursday Island.' He hands Leilani a small bottle of medicine and takes the last of Sario's coins. 'I'll need to observe her regularly and check her breathing over a longer period, and she will need further treatment. Bring her back every few days.'

The tall woman hands Sario another bill as they help Apu to the door. He's paid some bills. Now there's more! His head pounds with worry – there's no money left and Thaati hasn't come. How will he pay for more treatment?

The harbour is rocking with boats, and fishy smells are attracting squawking, hungry gulls as Sario makes his way out along the jetty to the packing shed. The first luggers are back and their catches unloaded.

He peers through the huge open doors and can't believe his eyes. Heaps of crusty pearl-shells as big as hospital plates are slipping and clattering onto the packing shed floor.

'It's a mighty start to the season!' a skipper shouts. Sario sighs with relief; his worries unwinding. He'll get dive work, he'll earn money. He'll learn to pump-dive, for certain! But he needs cash now – Apu can't wait for her medicine. Can he work here today? Scrub shells? Pack crates? He looks around for the boss man. No white faces anywhere.

and down onto the sandy beach and shore. They splash him with seawater, washing away blood and sticky bits of shell.

Sario lies in the shallows, bruised and sore, his wounds smarting from the sea salt. The sun filters hot and steamy through the grey monsoon clouds, but the water is cool – it revives him, refreshes his thoughts. Who *is* this Japee? Why is he so angry?

'Do you know that Japee?' Sario's eyes flash back to the packing shed at the end of the long jetty.

Wesley nods; he's heard the talk on Thursday Island. 'I bin workin' here since start of wet season, stockin' boats, sourcin' supplies and wantin' to leave TI,' he says. 'Him pump-diver, Hiroshi.'

'Hir-o-shi.' Spittle shoots from Sario's mouth as he sounds out the name, but he doesn't know it, he hasn't heard of this *mabaeg*. 'Too many Japees on the islands these days.'

'Bin listen white-fella talk,' Wesley adds. 'Hiroshi crack-diver. White-skipper fav'rit.'

'Bad Japee,' Lauro mutters. He's been listening to the Manila boys' stories; he's heard the rattle of fear in their voices. 'Japee is trouble.'

Sario catches his warning. The Japee's a bully for certain, and he wants to demonstrate his power for some reason. He's important, he's a pump-diver. He has the top job. But importance won't save him down in the deep. 'Danger is always lurking,' Sario mutters.

He rolls over in the shallows and tells the boys how his family suffers from diving. 'My apu struggles to breathe with damaged lungs, and my sister is deaf and in pain. Our cousins are lost to the sea somewhere, and now my thaati is out there diving who knows where.' But now *he's* got to find dive work, Sario says; he needs money to buy medicines for his mother and food for his family, they're a long way from their kin. He's experienced; he's been diving the Strait near his island since he was a small boy, in strong unpredictable currents, and on razor-sharp coral that shreds skin if a wave smashes you into the reef. 'Local knowledge is far more valuable than any Japee diver,' he adds.

The boys are around his age . . . thirteen, fourteen? 'Do you pump-dive?' he asks them.

'No,' Lauro fires back. He's adamant, his mind set firm; he'll *never* go down with a breathing-pipe. 'Devil lives down in the very deep!' He's seen pump-divers surface ghost-white with fear, trembling and incoherent, rambling about things they saw in the deep, horror in their vacant stares.

Sario dismisses his story. Lauro is a kind boy, but he seems too jumpy for a diver – afraid of his own shadow, easily intimidated. Doesn't he know that pump-divers earn more money – much more than swimming-divers, who can't stay under as long, or collect as much shell? Sario has never been deeper than six fathoms – he can't wait to walk the sea-floor in a diving suit and breathing helmet. His body has grown and his shoulders have broadened since the Coming of the Light celebrations; he won't slip out of the big copper helmet. And he needs reliable money, a good pay.

Wesley shakes his head. Blackfellas like him don't get the chance to wear a helmet and suit. 'No binghi pump-divin',' he says. 'Japee more importan' fella.'

Sario wonders why the Japanese consider themselves superior, and why white skippers prefer them.

'Japee dive all day, harves' more shell, make more money, white-fella say.'

'Who gets the money?' Sario wants to know. 'The Japees?' They're taking over Thursday Island with their Japee shops, Japee slipways – even a Japee bathhouse! 'Islanders are not getting rich from pearl-shell!' he snaps.

'Mudda-of-pearl valu'ble export.' Wesley repeats the numbers he's heard. 'One hun'red thousand pound a year!' He whistles and rolls his big black eyes. 'Plenty money this country.' The shell divers know that buyers in London pay a high price for mother-of-pearl from Torres Strait, and factories in Europe can't get enough to make buttons and ornaments and jewellery.

A gentle wave rolls in and Sario slaps the water with exasperation. 'Torres Islanders don't benefit!' He remembers his elders yarning about the loss of seafood and income, and how far they have to travel to harvest shells. *Japanese divers are taking our work, taking our livelihood. The sea feeds our families, it provides currency to trade – shell and* dhangal *and* waru. *Our riches are in the sea and others are looting it!*

Wesley's seen the Island-fellas gathering under palm trees, waving their arms in protest, but Island strife doesn't bother him. He wants more Japanese to come, then he can go home. 'More Japee, less work for black boys!' He doesn't want to be on this island or a pearling lugger; his tribe is on the mainland and he's plenty homesick. 'Go home to my mob. Big land 'cross water.'

The missionaries sent him to work on the boats, men who preached about light and hope. He sees no reward for his work – they collect his pay and use it to run their Mission School. 'No money, little food, dive long day,' he grumbles. Why would he stay here?

Most pearl-shell workers come from somewhere else – other islands, other countries. Many are forced here to work against their will, like him and Lauro.

Lauro aches for his family in the Philippines. Every night he sits crying and talking about his loved ones, about his loss. 'I go home soon, to Manila,' he says. And he'll do anything to get there, *anything* to make his dream come true.

He tells the boys how recruiters came and kidnapped him from his village. 'Big men – blackbirders.' They wrestled him from his mother's arms and threw her biscuits and trinkets in exchange. 'Lauro will return with lots of money,' they promised. But it wasn't true. They took strong, healthy boys to work, and white skippers paid them four pounds a boy.

'Labour abuse!' folk were shouting and protesting through the streets of London. 'Protect coloured people! Stop these greedy, lawless blackbirders.'

Some tried. The British Imperial Government introduced a law to stamp out blackbirding, but oceans are vast and difficult to patrol – black labour is plentiful and provides a cheap workforce.

'It's the Japees that bother me the most,' Sario says. 'Why are they so pushy and controlling?' He's been watching them on the dry dock. 'More irritating than a coral cut.' And now they're building boats and manning crews – soon they'll be flying Japee flags!

'Do you work for Japee skippers?' he asks.

'Sometimes.' Lauro nods. 'No one checks their dummy-licences.' All divers know that Asians are forbidden from holding a boat-licence under the Fisheries Act. 'Some Japees get around the law,' Lauro says, with a wink. 'They pay rent to white boat-owners and fish under their licences.' He admires their shrewdness. 'Licences are rarely checked, and the government boat *Pearl* doesn't call often.'

'Japee smart fella,' Wesley agrees. 'Him listen, him learn blackfella custom.'

Sario sits up, more confused than ever. Japees are taking work from island men, yet educating themselves at the same time? Learning island customs? Understanding Aboriginal cultures?

He stands slowly, his legs shaky, his thoughts in a muddle. He doesn't care where his boat-skipper comes from, or the colour of his skin, but he must be a fair man, not pushy like the white trader! He must pay with money – white-man's cash – not biscuits and tea. Food rations won't buy medicine for Apu.

Lauro sees Sario swaying unsteadily on his feet. 'Go home,' he offers. 'I'll wash the shells in the packing shed and clean away your blood.'

'*Eso.*' Sario is grateful; his walk home will be slow and painful enough. He'll go via the lagoon; the tide is out and fish could be trapped. Will fresh fish cheer Apu? He doesn't have money or rations to take home, only cuts and bruises and those nagging questions. *Who is Hiroshi? Why did he kick him in the ribs?*

Chapter Fourteen

Leilani rushes to help Sario when he staggers in weak and wounded. She takes the fish from his grip and eases him down gently onto a woven mat. She scoops a mug of water from the bucket and examines his cuts and bruises while he drinks. 'I will heal you, little *babat*.'

Sario stretches out on the pandanus mat and watches his sister get to work. Leilani will relieve his pain, she always does; her deafness has somehow strengthened her sense of touch and blessed her with healing hands. She bathes his cuts, then mixes her potions. All kinds of juices and sweet-smelling plants go into her mixing bowl – tree sap, bark and roots, wild-bee honey. She crushes herbs and seeds with a stone and makes a thick brown balm. She's taking her work so seriously, like her aunties, that Sario can't help but tease her.

'Your touch is so tender, big sister, I couldn't mend without you.' He winks and smiles. 'You're a *paekau*, a butterfly – your delicate wings dust and heal my wounds.'

Leilani reads his lips as she spreads the soothing balm over his chest wounds. She doesn't appreciate his mocking. Healing is not a game! Her remedies work, her treatments are effective. She'll show him! She takes a handful of fresh juicy leaves and squeezes them along his cuts. The sharp biting sap dribbles into his raw wounds. 'Is my healing delicate enough for you, little *babat*?'

'Owww.' Sario sits bolt upright.

'Good remedy, hah?' Leilani laughs, and clears away her mixing bowl.

She leaves him to rest and goes out to tend the vegetable garden. Every afternoon as the sun goes down she lets the fowls peck and scratch in the dirt while she fetches water and sprinkles the plants. She digs up a yam or cassava to cook in the coals of the fire and picks red chillies and green leafy herbs to eat with the fish. Waiben is a dry land and lacks fresh water, but her family won't starve here; there are coconuts and berries, fish and crabs. She misses her island home, her cousins and aunties who've taught her about plants and healing remedies, but Waiben has a white doctor and a proper cottage hospital, so it is the best place for Apu. And when Sario gets paid, there will be money to buy stronger medicines to clear her lungs and ease her chest pain.

Sario lies on the woven mat listening to his mother wheezing and coughing and trying to unblock her breathing passages. She's sitting out in the warm salty air inhaling vapours from a pot of steaming leaves, her only relief. He's her only son and a poor provider; Leilani is the better carer.

His guilt is worse than a hundred shell cuts. He's earned nothing again today. He hasn't even worked! What has he done? Collected a fish from the lagoon and been bullied by a Japee he doesn't even know!

Sario watches his mother shuffle in, her face gaunt, her chest sunken. She eases her bony frame down onto the mat and stares in shock at his injuries. 'Don't worry, Apu. I heal quickly,' he assures her. 'Leilani coat me in smelly ointment. She order me to rest.'

'Tell me, Sario.' She sits, waiting to hear the full story.

'I trip on sharp shells in the packing shed, that's all – a few cuts, nothing more.' He won't tell her about the cruel Japee with the lightning kick, or she'll worry even more.

'It's a huge haul, *gorsar* shells,' Sario prattles on, 'and it's only the start of the season, the spring tides.' He's yarning more in white talk and he thinks he sounds clever using new words about seasons and monsoons. He'll teach Esike when he gets back home. 'Only a few boats are back, and already pearl-shells are heaped high on the packing shed floor. I'll get work, don't worry.' There'll be more skippers looking for swimming-divers, for sure – but he wants to work on a pump-boat.

She studies the deep purple bruise spreading down his ribs and knows there is more to his story. 'Don't make trouble, Sario,' she warns. 'Skippers don't want fighters on their boats.' He's eager to work and earn money, but he has to stay alert. 'There are many dangers,' she adds. Strong, unpredictable currents that can drag a diver miles from his boat, menacing sharks, jealous divers and greedy skippers who care more for money than a diver's life. 'Luggers have to go much further now, out into deep dangerous waters. All the close shallow beds have been fished out, stripped of pearl-shell.' She pats his arm and says she will pray for his safe return.

In her day, she could wade out at low tide and collect shells from rock pools and mangroves, she could dive in less than a fathom of water, and pop back up with one or two shells. She would dive all day, every day – fill dinghies with pearl-shell. But there were greedy skippers in her time too, cruel men who wouldn't let her rest, who forced her to dive too deep and wouldn't allow her out of the water to eat. Now she suffers.

With his ribcage firmly strapped, Sario can move a little easier the following afternoon. He wanders up Green Hill to watch the sun go down, hoping the stifling heat will ease a little now the big yellow ball is slipping between the islands to the west: Gialug and Palilag, Friday Island and Goods Island. The dying rays are shimmering across the green-blue water, the palm trees are swaying, and the fat white pigeons flying down from New Guinea remind him of home. Is Esike out hunting them . . . or is he fishing from the rocks, or combing the shore for washed-up treasure? When will Apu be well enough to take home so he can see his cousins again, his uncles and aunties, his homeland?

The big iron cannons facing out to sea look harsh and out-of-place on the peaceful tropical island. *They've been put there to defend the Colony, to ward off attacks from Russian ships that might sail into the channel*, the crewman told him. But the Russians never came – Japee divers came instead! They swarmed over the Torres Strait, changing Islanders' lives. The soldiers should turn the big guns on them!

He's heard white skippers yarning about Federation, when the six colonies will unite and form one nation, the Commonwealth of Australia. Some skippers are keen for change, others against it. But what about the new law coming – to keep Australia white? Only white-skinned people will be allowed into the country. It's a good law. Japees will have to leave, Chinese, Malays and Indians. Torres Islanders will sell their pearl-shell and keep the money.

The sky darkens and so do his thoughts. What if black Australians are forced out too – his people, the Torres Strait Islanders? And Wesley's mob – the mainland binghis? Will they be dragged from their homes like Lauro? He shivers, uneasy. White Australia is a long way off . . . isn't it?

He thumps the wire fence as he leaves. He has his own battles to fight – and his Japee enemy is much closer.

Chapter Fifteen

'Come.' Lauro grabs Sario's arm and drags him towards the Shipping Master's Office, where a man is propping open the heavy wooden doors. 'Captain Greely needs a crew, swimming-divers.'

'Swimming-divers!' Sario pulls back. 'I want to pump-dive, wear a helmet and suit.'

'Maybe you will! Greely installed a pump in Sydney, on lay-up.'

Sario grins – his dream is possible. 'Imagine breathing underwater and walking the very deep.'

'It's foolish, Sario! Going down six fathoms is risky enough.' Lauro shakes his head. 'What if your air-pipe kinks and cuts off your air forty fathoms down?'

Sario shudders. It could happen, but he's not giving up; he'll follow his dream like the redhead sailor told him to . . . but who will teach him to pump-dive?

'Some pump-divers never come up!' Lauro adds, pushing Sario on to sign up. 'Stick with swimming-diving, where you're not so far from the surface.' Lauro's job is to muster a crew of swimming-divers, and he's keen to gain favour with Captain Greely . . . with *any* boat skipper who can sail him home to Manila. 'Greely pays his swimming-divers with cash, not food rations. Thirty shillings a month, maybe.'

The talk of money and a pump excites Sario – swimmers are often paid with food rations, flour, sugar, biscuits and tea. He needs cash and he wants to learn to pump-dive. Besides, Greely could be his last chance; most skippers have mustered a crew and left for the pearling grounds.

Wet season rain is spitting on the iron roof as they enter the Shipping Office. The clerk hands Sario a pen and watches as he signs the Terms of Agreement. He stamps the document and checks the date: *5th February, 1899*. 'You are articled to Captain Greely for a term of ninety days,' he says. 'You will work aboard the vessel *Sea Devil*.'

The boys leave the Shipping Office and hurry along the jetty. Sario can't wait to see Greely's lugger; his hopes are high it will be as sleek and neat as the white trader's lugger. Two smart vessels, *Pegasus* and *Evelyn*, are leaving port, their sails up, jibs pointing into the wind. *Sea Devil* is the only lugger left in the harbour, her two masts standing tall, her sharp bow roped to the long jetty that stretches out into the deep waters of Port Kennedy.

Sario fumes as he climbs aboard – she is dirty and dilapidated, alive with cockroaches. 'This no way to keep a boat!' He kicks aside a pile of rubbish. Why is she not fresh with paint after lay-up? Any captain worth his salt would keep his boat shipshape. 'Who is this white man, Captain Greely?'

Lauro shrugs, he doesn't know. He's only met the captain this morning and been given the job of finding divers and loading provisions. Now he'll have to find a way to distract Sario – keep his mind off the lugger's rundown state. 'We'll kill the cockroaches,' Lauro giggles. He's played the game before, it's fun. 'We'll knock 'em flat with tins of treacle and jam.' He drops a heavy tin on one roach to demonstrate. 'They move slowly in the sunlight, we'll count 'em as they drown. Highest number wins!' He laughs and tosses the brown roach overboard.

Time passes quickly, cleaning, painting, banging in nails and filling the water barrels. The boys flatten dozens of the big brown crawlies as they stow supplies, but they've lost count of the number. Sario scrubs the cabin and galley and packs away tins of corned beef and salt-pork. He stacks firewood in the hold below deck.

Wesley stows jars of pickles and syrup, bottles of vinegar and sauce. He fills the slop-chest with new items, luxury goods that crew members can purchase. Blankets. Tobacco. Confectionery. Shirts.

Lauro fills the dinghy with dry goods. Rice. Sugar. Tea. Salt. Flour. Onions. Matches. At the end of the day, he throws a canvas sheet over the provisions and looks around for Sario to help him rope it down.

Sario is below deck in the hold, his attention on the diving-pump – a tall wooden box with air-pressure gauges and two large iron wheels, one either side with a handle for turning. He examines the pump closely, his bare feet straddling a large coil of rubbery pipe that feeds out the bottom. How does the contraption work? How does it pump air through the pipe and down into a diver's helmet underwater?

He doesn't figure it out, he doesn't get the chance. A heavy drum of kerosene crashes down from the deck above, smashing his foot and pinning him to the floor. He bellows and shoves the weight off his foot, five sloshing gallons of it. He looks at his bleeding, throbbing toes. Where did the kero drum come from? All supplies have been stowed in lockers or roped down.

A Kanaka man hears him scream and runs to help. He lifts Sario up through the hatch and sits him gently on the deck, his back against the cabin. Sario's foot is swelling, his anger too. 'Is there a Japee in this crew?' he bellows at the South Sea Island man.

The Kanaka nods and hurries off. 'Find bandage. Wrap foot.'

Sario looks around. Is the Japee involved this time?

The Kanaka returns with a strip of cloth and a thin wooden chopstick. He snaps the stick into three short pieces and fits the splints carefully between Sario's swollen toes.

Sario studies the South Sea Island man. He's a hard worker, his arms thick and muscly, a finger missing, and skin much darker than Sario's. 'Is your village a long way from Torres Strait?'

The Kanaka nods. 'A long sea journey.'

'You swimming crew?'

'I'm the tender.' His dark eyes light with pride; it's a responsible job, tending the pump-diver and keeping him safe down in the deep.

'Is your pump-diver a Japee?' Sario asks.

The Kanaka nods. 'Hiroshi,' he says. 'Crack-diver.'

Sario grits his teeth and groans; there's no chance of pump-diving now. The Japee won't teach him – he wouldn't even ask! But he needs to pump-dive to earn better money! Swimming-divers earn less than thirty shillings a month, and the doctor says Apu has to return to hospital regularly. She has pleurisy, he said, and she will need to have the fluid drained from her lungs. On top of the medical bills he has to pay the store for food – Leilani can't fish if she's helping Apu day and night. Then he has to earn money to buy tools for his clan. And save for their island lugger!

'Be still!' the Kanaka snaps, trying to tie the ends of the bandage.

But Sario can't stop his nervous twitching – his anger, his pain, his worry. Tears well in his eyes. He hasn't received a penny since the Japee kicked him in the ribs.

The Kanaka helps him gently to his feet. 'Toes mend straight now, all strapped tight.'

But Sario's in no mood for smiles. Now that he's standing he can see the Japee running back along the jetty, his long black hair swishing over his shoulders. He should drop five gallons on *his* foot! Shove *him* onto a pile of sharp shells!

'Come, brudda.' Wesley hoists Sario onto his back. 'Piggyback home.'

It will be less painful than hobbling all the way, but what will Apu say when he arrives with no money for medicine? They'd expected he would earn a little cash today in the packing shed. At least he has money coming from his day on *Sea Devil* – and he has work ahead. His diving pay will be waiting at the end of the trip when he signs off. But it won't be enough!

Wesley shuffles home slowly, Sario heavy on his back. As he passes the Thursday Island Hotel, he nods to a grubby whitefella asleep on the pub veranda. 'Him cap'in. Him drunk.'

A sour smell wafts from the hotel: stale ale and cigarettes, a whiff of vomit. Sario shudders. Tomorrow he'll be sailing with this crew. A drunken captain, a cruel Japanese, and a Kanaka tender who idolises his Japee diver. And all aboard a roach-infested wreck! It's worse; he suddenly realises. 'Tomorrow is Friday!'

Wesley stiffens at the words – he knows the old sea superstition and it terrifies him. It rattles every sailor. *Leave port on a Friday – bring bad luck!*

Chapter Sixteen

Leilani and Apu wave him off in the dark. 'We be alright,' Leilani assures him. '*Uzari*, go.' She smiles encouragement.

Sario is nervous and excited. Now that the boys have patched the old hull, filled her cracks, scrubbed her decks and stocked the galley with food, he's hoping *Sea Devil* holds up in rough seas. But what will Greely be like? Pushy and bullying like the white trader?

He waits patiently on the jetty, clutching a basket woven from banana leaves and listening for his call to climb aboard. Another figure stands further along, indistinct in the dim dawn light.

Shadows move on the deck below, dark blurry shapes. The boat timbers creak and groan with the strain of the mooring ropes.

'Come aboard!' The words whisk past him on the wind.

Sario moves to the ladder and turns his back to climb down. He takes a step, his foot on the first rung.

'Not you!'

Japee accent! Sario peers down, his insides tightening along with the mooring ropes.

'You!' The Japee beckons the other person waiting on the jetty. 'Come!'

A boy hurries to the ladder, a blanket-roll under his arm. Sario can see his face clearly now – Japanese! He grips the sides of the ladder, his fingernails digging into his palms. His dive job is slipping away . . . the money . . . Apu's medicine. He won't let it go. He can't!

On the deck, he can see faces emerging from the shadows, their dark features becoming more distinct with the sun's first light – Wesley, Lauro, the Kanaka – familiar faces, offering encouragement.

'I'm signed on this lugger,' Sario shouts down, ensuring his voice will be heard above the wind. 'I'm articled to Captain Greely of *Sea Devil*.' His palms are sweaty, his grip slippery on the steel ladder.

'Move away!' the Japee orders.

Sario takes a deep breath and climbs down, his basket bumping over the metal rungs with him. 'Coming aboard, captain!' he calls.

The grubby man appears on deck, rubbing his eyes, half-asleep. 'Who's making this racket?'

'Him!' Hiroshi turns on Sario, his finger pointed, his eyes wild with accusation.

Sario swings away, the Japee's long fingernail an inch from his nose and sharp as a spear. He ducks, and drops into the boat – into a sea of concerned faces.

Wesley elbows his way from the back of the group, and plants his feet firmly in front of Greely. 'Island boy good diver, cap'in. We sail now? All crew aboard.'

'No!' Hiroshi folds his arms in defiance. 'He come!' He nods to the nervous boy on the top of the ladder. 'Japee boy. Better diver.'

Greely turns away, hungry for his breakfast and disinterested in the Japee's carry-on. He peers into Sario's basket. 'What did you bring? Coconut pudding? Cassava sweets?' He likes Islanders' tasty treats.

'Cockroach baits,' Sario answers, and steps back. The white skipper stinks of cigarettes, sweat, and stale liquor – a smell worse than dead fish. He reaches into his basket and takes out a small green spongy bundle. 'It's my sister's recipe – flour, sugar, borax.' Leilani has rolled little balls of mixture in banana leaves and bound them tight with vine. 'Roaches will eat these and die. You'll be rid of the pests.'

Greely throws his head back and laughs, a loud roaring snort, his belly wobbling under his open shirt. He slaps Sario on the back. 'You show initiative, boy! I like that.'

Sario's grin tightens – he'll need more than cockroach baits to rid this wreck of pests!

'Set sail, boys!' Greely shouts.

Sario glances at Hiroshi. The Japee stares back, his eyes narrowing into evil slits, the veins in his neck bulging – thick as deck-rope. Most Japees control their feelings to avoid embarrassment, but not this one.

Sea Devil's decks are crammed. Sario has to clamber over buckets and nets and crates of supplies to reach the dark holes and crevices and plant his cockroach baits. Lauro helps him. 'Greely didn't lay up his boat for repairs,' he says. 'Smart skippers submerge their luggers in seawater while they're on lay-up, and drown the pests.'

'Greely sailed her to Sydney instead, to get the pump installed.' Sario is delighted.

The wind gusts fill her sails, and *Sea Devil* pushes north over the choppy white peaks on her long voyage. Sario looks forward with excitement; he might see his uncles and cousins fishing in the canoe. He might see Esike dragging washed-up treasures along the beach. He might see his thaati, back home again.

Waiben, the biggest pearling-station in the Torres Strait, is dropping away, a speck in the ocean. Wesley blinks back tears. His people are a long way south now, and he's sailing further from them – far from the bush tucker and ceremonies, far from the rhythm of his land. 'My mob back there,' he cries.

'Don't look back!' Lauro warns. 'It's bad luck.' He is only looking forward from now on – to when he's back home in Manila with his family.

Wesley sniffs and wipes his eyes. He'd escape if he could, he'd go walkabout, go home. But it's impossible, he knows. 'White-man come along. Hunt you out. Send you to work.' He works hard and asks for little and still he's at the bottom of the colour heap – lower than Kanakas, lower than Lauro and the Manila boys, even lower than Sario and the Torres Strait Island fellas. The Aborigines Protection Act doesn't change a thing.

'I never learn horse or bullock or station,' he says. He didn't get the chance. 'Learn boat, learn sea; learn big-fella tides.' He's a good sailor, he can read the weather, but his heart is back on the mainland. 'Hollow out tree, make canoe and palm-leaf sail. Wind carry me home.' Every night he dreams of his homeland, of hunting goanna and tracking dingo. Mission school is not for him. *Plant seeds. Read Bible*, mission-fella say. *Learn gospel, garden and God.*

Recruiters came ashore with tobacco, alcohol and sugar; they bribed tribal elders with addictive treats that would keep them supplying workers. '*Good boy, help everyone*, mission-fella say.' They sent him to work on the boats and kept his pay.

'Some binghi run away. Take dinghy and stores, make way back to mob,' Wesley says. 'They be caught. Magistrate say, *Refuse to work? Go lock-up. Six weeks.*' He'd run away too, if he could – but not to lock-up.

Sario is different. He loves the sea and diving; saltwater runs through his veins like fibre through a coconut.

He'll work hard this trip. He'll show Greely he's a good diver, a willing worker, not a lazy slug – not one to be kicked and bullied. He'll be as strong as a warrior and Thaati will be proud. And at the end of the trip his pay will be waiting – enough to pay Leilani's food store bill and some medical bills. But if he could somehow learn to pump-dive, he'd earn much more – enough to pay all the bills, buy cloth for Leilani to sew, buy tools for the old people. He licks the salt spray from his lips and stows his troubles away. He could even save a bit for their lugger!

Wesley glances around the deck at his companions, a mix of skin-colours and cultures, all nationalities mixed in together like lugger food – meat, vegetables and rice. 'Company rice,' he says, with a grin. They will share their stories and customs, he likes that. He looks at Hiroshi . . . what is the Japee up to? His eyes are focused on Sario, burning like firesticks into Sario's back. Wesley turns away with a prickle of fear. Hiroshi bad-fella!

Chapter Seventeen

Sario wakes early, the lugger rocking with the change of tide. He crawls over the deck, over boys sleeping through the motion, and reaches a spot where he can stand and stretch. He leans out over the gunnel, where paint has worn away, and empties his bladder. The breeze is light.

'Ten to fifteen knots – it's a good day for diving,' Cook says. He squats, toasting bread on an iron grille and juggling a steaming kettle, his cooking flame guarded by a cut-down oil drum – a fire at sea is his greatest fear.

Greely is below deck in the hold, dismantling the diving-pump and cursing loudly at the pump-boys. 'Hold the lantern high and shine some decent light!'

Hiroshi uncoils his air-pipes and lays them out along the deck. He examines each section carefully for kinks and worn patches – any fault that could prevent air getting down to him underwater.

Sario watches the Japee from the cabin roof, his small blanket pulled tight around his shoulders. He'll learn everything he can about breathing-pipes and air-pumps, but he won't be going down in a helmet now – the Japee won't teach him. He eats his toast and drinks his tea – his breakfast light before diving.

'Get the dinghy in the water!' Greely bellows from below deck. 'The pump isn't working, so only swimming-divers down today.' He rushes up the ladder. 'You two join them.' He hustles the pump-hands along. 'Conditions are good, a neap tide; little movement.'

Sario climbs into the dinghy with Wesley, Lauro and the pump-boys. The pump-hands won't be needed on board today. Nor will the pump-diver. Hiroshi steps into the dinghy and takes up the oars. He's in charge. Sario swallows and turns away.

They row into shallower waters, the dinghy gliding silently over the calm sea, the coral reef below coming alive with bursts of colour as the sun's rays penetrate the green-blue water. Pink coral flowers. Purple. Green. Soft yellow corals waving long graceful ribbons. Orange fish nibbling. Blue fish darting. Sario studies the islands in the distance, small dark lumps on the ocean. He spots a fishing canoe. Is it Esike and his uncles? Thaati? It's a tiny speck on the water, too far away to know.

Splash! They jump in the water together; swimming-divers always go in a group to scare off any sharks. A tall tower of water shoots up over the dinghy. They giggle as they surface. Hiroshi is standing dripping wet and unamused – as stiff and wooden as a warning beacon.

The boys take a deep breath, fill their lungs with air and kick down, two or three fathoms to the bottom, their naked bodies making shadowy ripples. Pearl-oysters grow on the leeward side of the reef away from the wind. Sario skims the mud quickly with his toes, feeling for hard shells. Slugs. Sponges. Sea-stars. Shell! He snatches up three and kicks to the surface. The pearl-shells are beauties, the size of Greely's dinner bowls. He pitches them into the dinghy.

He fills his lungs and swims down again.

Up, down, up he goes, hour after hour until he grows weak with hunger and numb with cold. He reaches for the stern of the dinghy to rest and catch his breath. He clings on, his heart thumping, his head pounding.

'Dive!' Hiroshi bellows. 'Dawn till dusk!' He pushes Sario down under the water, and holds him there with force.

Sario struggles, his air dwindling. He tries to prise the Japee's fingers from his head, but all his strength is gone. He drops low in the water and slips from the Japee's grasp, out of his reach. He kicks to the surface, gasping for air, his chest heaving. He reaches for the dinghy and runs his hand up the timber planks until his fingers curl over the thick rim. His grip is weak, his fingers wet and slippery.

'Dive!' Hiroshi prises his fingers from the dinghy and bends them back.

'*Owww.*' The pain is so cruel Sario can't bear it. He lets go and swaps hands. His fingers are throbbing and his sore hand is useless, dangling like fish bait in the water.

'Dive!' *Whack! Whack!* 'Raise more shell!'

Sario's knuckles are bleeding and swelling. He sees the heavy wooden oar coming down again to smash them. He lets go and drops below the surface, exhausted, Hiroshi's face wavering above him. Sario swims under the dinghy and rises silently on the other side, keeping low in the water close to the bow.

Wesley and Lauro surface nearby. Sario watches them pitch shells into the dinghy with a clattering racket. He signals them to toss him in too – in with the pearl-shells.

Thump! He lands heavily, scattering the pile of crusty hard shells, but he's too weary to care. The Japee is hanging over him, a cigarette in his mouth.

Hiroshi draws deeply on the cigarette, his lips sucking back, his cheeks hollow, and blows the smoke in Sario's face – a long stinking stream.

Sario gags and chokes. His nose blocks, his eyes sting, his head spins. He blacks out.

Chapter Eighteen

What does the Japee want? Sario is puzzled; he has nothing to give him, he holds no power. 'More Japees on Waiben than white men,' he complains to the Kanaka as they open shells on the back deck. 'The island is swamped with them.'

The Kanaka grins. 'They call the east side Jap Town. Boarding houses at the bottom of Milman Hill are packed full.'

Sario smiles. He likes the South Sea Island tender; they work well together. Greely barked the orders. *Stay out of the water and settle your breathing. Work with the tender, shelling*. But Greely didn't reprimand the Japee. Unfair!

Sario rams the blade of his knife between the fleshy lips of an oyster shell and twists to prise it apart. He cuts away the meaty lump inside, the soft muscle that holds the shell halves together, and breaks the hinge. The two shiny, iridescent surfaces glint in the sunlight, rainbow colours – mother-of-pearl.

'Most Japees are polite, self-respecting men, they keep to themselves,' the Kanaka said. He gathers the empty shells and stacks them in a pile. 'Most like to gamble their money.'

Gambling? Is that Hiroshi's problem? Sario shakes his head and wonders. Is the Japee such a fool, to waste his pay? 'Why do Japanese want to dominate and push us around?' he complains. 'Soon Japee luggers will be trawling the Torres Strait hauling up *all* our shell!' He rolls his eyes at the thought of it. 'Japees should stop pushing Islanders about and go back to Japan – back to their tea-houses and lantern ceremonies.' He'd been told about their customs. 'And they can take their stinking garlic and ginger with them!'

Sario hears Hiroshi down in the hold arguing with Greely, telling him how to fix the pump. He smiles. Wesley rowed off and left the Japee behind this morning – on purpose. He left early with the swimming-divers, as silent as a sunbeam.

'I respect Japees for their hard work and efficiency,' the Kanaka says, ignoring the arguing. 'But I don't like their domineering ways. They're arrogant, high-and-mighty.'

Sario nods. Most Islanders feel the same way.

'White pearlers think Japanese divers are indispensable, so they give them more benefits and pay them more money, and manipulate the law to keep them here!'

The Kanaka tosses his shell on the pile. 'It's unfair! Islanders are available to do the work.' He knows the value of opportunity, of getting a chance in life – he's come a long way from his South Sea village to improve himself. 'My people are skilled traders, we are used to dealing with white men,' he says, 'but we don't always approve of their ways.'

He's working his way up in pearl-fishing, and proud of his progress. 'First I am a swimming-diver, then a sheller, and pump-hand. Now I am tender.' He has importance; attending to a pump-diver is a well-respected position. 'I can sail the lugger and do any job now.'

Sario smiles, in awe of the Kanaka's rise. 'I want to learn to pump-dive,' he says. 'But the Japee hates me, he'd never teach me.'

'You are a threat to him.'

'A threat? To the Japee?' Sario is baffled.

'You raise more shell than the other boys. You're a good diver, a strong swimmer.'

'I can't even pump-dive!' Sario laughs.

The Kanaka picks up another shell and chips away at the rough brown edges and barnacle growth. 'Hiroshi will be shamed if you dive deeper than him and raise more shell.'

'Shamed?' Sario stares back at him in shock. 'I'd like to see that!' He prises open another shell, drops the oyster meat in a bucket and rinses the shell halves in another, swirling them in the dirty grey seawater. The Kanaka's words intrigue him. Is the Japee afraid of *him*? Afraid he'll take his job?

'In Japan it is not good to lose face, it is a sign of weakness,' the Kanaka continues. 'Respect and prestige are most important.'

'He should go back there, then!' Sario fires back. 'He has prestige, he's important now.'

The Kanaka stands and picks up the bucket of oyster flesh. 'Hiroshi will not go willingly.' He takes the bucket to the lugger's rigging and hangs the small thick muscle pieces over the ropes to dry in the sun.

Sario's mouth waters at the thought of eating the tasty meat later, when Cook fries it with onions.

'Japanese migrants are flowing into this country at a great rate,' the Kanaka continues. 'Some people want them banned, excluded. No Asiatics. They want to keep the colony British, a white Australia.' He picks up another shell and knifes it open. 'But it's not so straightforward. Australia is ruled by Britain, and Britain is an ally of Japan.'

'Send the Asians home!' Sario says, his mind made up . . . although he isn't too sure about the White Australia rule. No one in his family has white skin.

'You don't get a say in the matter – coloureds don't get a vote.'

How would he vote, if he could? He doesn't want Japees in the country, but he doesn't want Islanders tossed out with them. 'Australia should be for all Australians, black and white, everyone equal, no matter their colour.' But he can't imagine it – ever.

'Hiroshi can't go home. He's indentured labour,' the Kanaka says. 'His passage was paid with borrowed money. Now he has to work and pay back his debt in Japan.'

'I'm not stopping him earning money. Why does he pick on me?'

'He's worried. You could take his job, his wages and prestige. You know the Torres Strait waters, Sario, and you're a good strong diver.'

'I'd take his job and his money, if I could!' Sario grins.

'Hiroshi is not a competent swimmer. He was seasick when he first arrived, he'd never been on a boat before. You bother him, Sario. In Japan he was a poor noodle-seller, working the streets. Imagine his shame if he had to return?'

Chapter Nineteen

'The pump is working,' Greely yells. 'Get the Japee down. There's five hours of daylight left.'

The Kanaka drops his shell and scurries to the foredeck to dress Hiroshi. Sario continues shelling, a monotonous job without the tender's chatter to distract him. The storage areas are filling, so he stows some shells in the cabin, under the captain's bunk on the starboard side, and some port side under the Japee's bed – pearl side down. The tender and Cook sleep on the upper bunks.

'Hope you don't mind the stink of rotting oyster-flesh under your bed,' Sario says, watching Cook drop his fishing line over the side. 'It's impossible to dig out every bit of meat.' At least at night he breathes fresh air sleeping on the deck. The timber deck is hard and cramped with bodies, and wet and uncomfortable when rain blows in, but he prefers it. Who would want to sleep in the cabin with Greely and the Japee?

'I'm used to fishy smells,' Cook says, pulling in his line. He's from a poor fishing village in the Philippines. 'I've fished all my life.'

Except for the smell, it isn't a problem leaving tiny scraps of meat. The shells will be scrubbed again thoroughly back at the packing shed. They'll be weighed and graded and packed in wooden crates stencilled *M-O-P SYDNEY*. The mother-of-pearl will go first to Sydney, then on to London.

Cook hauls up a shiny silver trevally and jiggles the hook from its mouth. 'Two more this size and we'll have a hearty supper.' He looks around, checking to make sure the diver is still on deck, then baits his hook again. His heavy sinker takes it down quickly.

It's difficult to open shells and watch the long process of dressing the diver at the same time, but Sario is not going to look away and miss anything. First the Japee puts on a flannel vest and woollen cap to protect his skin. Then the tender helps him into the bulky diving suit and tightens the leather straps. Hiroshi sits on a wooden box so the tender can buckle his heavy leather boots, the thick soles and toecaps weighted with lead to stop him floating up from the sea-floor.

Next to go on is a brass corselet with a neck-stand and screw holes. This sits on the Japee's shoulders like heavy metal armour, and the tender places extra lead weights on top. He screws down the big copper breathing helmet tightly, to prevent water getting in. Hiroshi inches his way to the side of the boat. It's a slow shuffle, his diving suit awkward and cumbersome. The tender loops a short rope to his corselet and hooks on a canvas bag to hold the shells.

'*Ouch!*' Sario jumps and drops his knife. He was so engrossed he's sliced his thumb. Blood runs down his fingers and drips onto the clean shells at his feet. He plunges his hand in the rinsing bucket, the dirty grey water swirling with oyster scraps.

Cook moves quickly. He winds his fishing line round a wooden cleat to secure it and tips the filthy water overboard. He scoops up clean seawater and dunks Sario's hand, washing the cut thoroughly. He tears strips from the tail of his shirt and binds the thumb tightly, to stop the bleeding.

'*Eso.*' Sario is grateful to Cook for his quick thinking. 'I'm not lucky. Another injury, another scar.'

Cook pulls the fishing line in quickly as the Kanaka tender helps Hiroshi over the side and onto the rope ladder.

'You two!' Greely shouts to Cook and Sario. 'Operate the pump!'

Sario jumps up and follows Cook to the bow, close on his heels with excitement. The pump-hands won't be back from diving until sundown; by then he'll know how to work the pump.

They climb down into the big open hatch and Cook tells him to turn the large iron wheels. Sario sees how the piston rods move up and down and pump air into the storage box. 'This is an air-pressure gauge.' Cook taps a round glass dial and they watch the needle flicker. 'It shows the volume of air pumped through the breathing-pipe and down into a diver's helmet.'

The Kanaka stands on the deck above, holding a rope. 'This is the diver's lifeline,' he calls down to Sario. 'Hiroshi tugs it to signal me.'

Hiroshi takes the rope and slips under the water, checking that his lifeline and breathing-pipe are floating freely and not tangled. Beside him is a taut rope, the depth-sounding line weighted with lead at the bottom.

'The tags woven into the rope indicate the depth of the water,' Cook explains. 'It's thirty fathoms here in this spot.' Sario nods. He's seen a depth-sounding line on the steamship.

They keep a regular rhythm turning the big wheels and pumping air down to Hiroshi, checking the pressure needle constantly to ensure he is getting enough air. The space is hot and confined and few breezes reach them. Sario's bare back prickles and itches with sweat. His arms ache and his bandaged thumb gets in the way of the wheel, but if he stops turning the Japee will die down there. Hiroshi's life is in his hands.

The tender peers over the side, waiting anxiously for a message on the lifeline; his responsibility immense. He holds the rope loosely, his fingers tuning in to the diver's movements far below. His jaw muscles twitch with concern, but he knows the rules. *Stay alert. Interpret signals. Make quick decisions.*

Sario is impatient to learn the rope signals. 'Is there a code?'

'A shake means he's all right. Two tugs, more air. Four tugs, haul up. Seven tugs, danger.' The tender quietens; he's tense. Only the waves slapping the hull break the silence.

Finally he feels a shake on the line. *All right.*

The crew settles into the flow of routine and Greely snores all afternoon.

Late in the day, the pump-hands return from diving and take over the wheel. Sario goes back to shelling. His pile is growing; the dinghy returned half-full of shell and the Japee is sending up heavy bags from the bottom.

Cook goes off to clean his catch. 'No fish guts overboard,' he says, with a nod. 'Diver still down.'

Sario shudders. Not even his worst enemy deserves to be ripped apart by monster jaws. But the Japee had better surface soon – daylight is fading, and dusk is feeding time for sharks on the reef.

Later, when Hiroshi is back on board and drinking tea, Sario feels a small hard pebble tucked in the folds of the oyster flesh. His hands tremble as he digs it out. The pearl is smooth with a cream lustre, reflecting the light from the pale quarter-moon. He closes his fingers over it to hide it from view; only one oyster-shell in a thousand holds a pearl. It forms when a tiny irritant slips inside the shell, a worm or a grain of sand, and the pearl-oyster wraps it up, cocooning the tiny intruder in nacre, layer after layer, and shaping a hard little pearl. They are clever little oysters! He'd bind his enemy up the same way, if he could.

Should he hand the pearl in to Greely? Is there a strict rule? The head diver usually claims the pearls but Hiroshi isn't getting his hands on this one! Who will know? Sario fetches his blanket and ties the tiny pearl in one corner. He knots the other three corners the same, hoping his little pearl isn't noticed.

He wipes his clammy hands down his blanket. Is it wrong to keep something that isn't his, to hide it away? The little pearl could save his mother's life! He could sell it and buy medicine. That would be fair, wouldn't it? Who owns the pearls in the ocean anyway? The oysters?

Wesley and Lauro secure the dinghy and set about clearing the decks for supper. They coil ropes, empty buckets and wind in the fishing lines. Cook peels the thick brown skin off a cassava and chops the tuber into short lengths. He drops the pieces into a pot of water and sets it to boil on the fire.

'No greens, no papaya fruit,' Lauro moans. His belly is upset and gassy. He longs for fresh greens and fruit, but fresh food doesn't keep long at sea. 'We could all be struck down with scurvy!' Then he'd never get home to Manila.

Wesley wants fish for his tucker, not vegetables and fruit. 'Carry banana on boat . . . catch no fish.' He knows *all* the old sea superstitions.

Meals are small and never enough for the hungry divers. Tonight they'll get a small serving of trevally and a taste of pearl-meat if they're lucky – if the important crew don't gobble it up first. Occasionally they'll anchor close enough to an estuary to bait the traps and get a feed of crab meat.

Sario holds out his plate for his share of oyster meat. He deserves a good scoop; he's been cutting the chewy flesh from shells all day and hanging it to dry on the rigging. He imagines the taste in his mouth, the salty flavour on his tongue. Cook holds the pan out to serve him, but Hiroshi swoops in and scrapes the lot into his bowl – every last scrap.

'*Burum*, pig!' Sario shouts. His fists fly up. His tin plate crashes to the deck. He'll knock the Japee overboard! He'll drown the smug pig!

Wesley grabs his shoulders and drags him back. 'Japee main man,' he warns. 'Big trouble, brudda.' Sario's fists keep flying, his temper boiling, but Wesley catches his wrists and holds them tight. 'Strike Japee, go lock-up long time.'

Sario pulls away and flings him off. But Wesley is right – if he strikes the Japee he'll be thrown off the lugger, and he might never work again. His mother's words come floating back. *Don't make trouble, Sario. Skippers don't want fighters on their boats.*

He snatches up a bucket of seawater and tips it over his head. He fills it again and again, bucket after drenching bucket raining down on him, dousing his anger and flooding the deck. He's dug out pearl-meat all day long – and he didn't even get a taste! 'Unfair!' he bellows.

Sario curls up in his blanket and feels for the hard little lump in the corner. He rolls the pearl in his fingers. What is it worth? It's a teardrop shape, a baroque pearl, not as valuable as the perfectly round pearls, but a gem to him. He'll trade for money; get cash in exchange. The Japee won't get his hands on it.

The anchor lamp swings dimly at the top of the mast and a few stars shine through the heavy monsoon clouds. It's late February, but he can make out parts of Tagai's canoe in the constellation, the tiny stars of his sword twinkling his direction home. He can't wait for Apu to get better so they can all return to their homeland. But today was a good day, as bright as the stars. He found a pearl, he's worked the pump; he's learnt a few rope signals and knows how to dress a diver. But then the greedy pig stole his pearl-meat!

Could he really shame the Japee? Bring him ill fortune? He would if he could. He'd ship him back to Japan, back to his noodle stall!

Chapter Twenty

'Shark!' Sario screams as he hits the surface. '*Kursi*, hammerhead!' He swims for his life, the wind whipping his words away. He can see the dinghy through the rain . . . further away than he thought. Hiroshi is standing trying to balance the rocking dinghy. He's in charge again, the sea too murky for pump-diving.

Is that a boy in the water? Lauro? Sario battles through the thundering waves, the sky grumbling and darkening overhead. He screams. 'No! Don't go down!' Where are the others? Sharks attack when a diver is rising.

His body is heavy and slow as a dugong, dragging through the lumpy sea. Every breath's a struggle. 'Shark!' His voice is weak; he's exhausted. He waited too long on the bottom, watching the shark, waiting for it to leave. It didn't go far. It's still here . . . somewhere in the dark murky water.

Lauro spots Sario on the crest of a wave, his arm in the air, waving. 'Something is wrong!' He looks to Hiroshi for instructions.

'Rough sea. It's nothing.' Hiroshi pushes Lauro down. 'Get more shell. Last chance.'

Wesley surfaces and hurls his shell into the dinghy. Sario spots him, his dark head tossing like a coconut in the waves. He has to stop him . . . or he'll go down again! Sario pushes on, gulping air, huge waves slamming into him. 'Shark!' he shrieks, as he gets closer. 'Get in!'

They scramble in together headfirst, the waves crashing and pounding the small boat. Hiroshi tries to balance the dinghy, his legs astride the wooden seat, as she pitches about in the rolling sea.

The pump-boys surface. 'Shark!' Sario yells, beckoning the young divers. 'Get in!' But they're already swimming for their lives.

The dinghy sits low in the water, heavy with shell and crowded with wet, shivering bodies. *Where is Lauro?* Sario peers into the water, his teeth chattering, rain peppering his body. He crosses his arms and rubs at his goosebumps. The water is dark and agitated. How long has his friend been under?

A sudden swirl. Round and round. Dark explosive circles. Blood red.

He's gone. Sario tightens his arms over his heaving chest. His tears flow with the rain. The kind boy from Manila will never make it home.

'It's your fault!' Sario turns on Hiroshi. 'You forced him down. Now he's gone!'

'Sad.' Hiroshi lowers his eyes. 'Good boy, good diver.'

Sario snatches up an oar. 'Shells! Money! That's all you care about. Your percentage of the catch!' He prods Hiroshi with the oar. He'll push *him* over! He'll send *him* down to the shark! Does Greely know the Japee's so cruel and money-hungry?

'No, brudda!' Wesley grabs the oar and holds it tight. But Sario is strong; pushing against him. 'Strike Japee, go lock-up!' Wesley warns, his face twisting with the strain of holding Sario back. 'Prison. Long time.' Wesley swings the oar with all the force he can muster.

Sario flies back over the wooden seat and lands on the hard, sharp shells, rain stinging his bare body. The pump-boys leap on him and hold him there, legs and arms wriggling like sea snakes.

'Greedy pearlers!' Sario screeches. 'They want more shell, they want more money. They gamble with our lives!'

Wesley takes up the oars and rows back to the lugger. It's a slow, treacherous journey through a rolling, mountainous sea, the dinghy full and Sario's behaviour erratic.

'Who cares about us black boys?' Sario shrieks. 'We dice with death!'

The air falls solemn, the divers upset and deep in thought.

Sario stumbles onto the lugger. 'We've lost the Manila-boy,' he cries, his heart as heavy as dive-boots. 'A hammerhead.'

Greely peers into the dinghy and surveys the haul of shell, little expression on his face.

'We risk our lives when we enter their territory,' the Kanaka says, shaking his head. 'Every diver encounters a shark at some time.'

'The Japee forced him down!' Sario snaps. 'I waved a warning and the Manila-boy saw me.' He curls up on the deck and pulls his blanket over his head. 'I'm not unloading the shell.'

Greely swigs his rum bottle and considers his next move. His divers are traumatised – he'll get no more work from them. The weather is blowing up, and there's worse to come. He's had five good days of a neap tide and decent shell hauls, despite problems with the pump. 'Lash down the dinghy!' he shouts. 'Head for TI.' It'll be a rough trip back, but he'll unload the catch, report the Manila-boy's death, and venture out when the seas improve.

'Go drown yourself,' Sario sobs into his blanket.

A heavy weight crashes down on his legs. He hears the shells rattle as the bucket lands. *Don't react! The Japee wants confrontation, he wants to demonstrate his authority. He wants an audience.* Sario stays huddled and still, a crab in its shell. He won't throw off his blanket, he won't yell and scream. He won't give *him* the satisfaction.

The boys sit rocking back and forth, alone with their thoughts, crying and contemplating. It could have been any one of them down in the depths, fighting the monster – dicing with death.

When *Sea Devil* passes over the waters where the diver disappeared, the boys stand and link arms, bowing their heads in respect, dressed neat and tidy in trousers and shirts. Sario's calico wrap flies at half-mast above. He leans over the side and lowers his empty banana basket into the sea, the one that held the cockroach baits. 'Let it carry you to a better world, Manila-boy. Safe *iawai*, journey.'

Chapter Twenty-One

Their journey back to Waiben is long and slow through the wild, bucking sea, the currents unpredictable and dangerous to navigate. Greely steers by the stars and his old compass. The boys point out coral reefs and sand cays, warning-beacons and rock formations, any hazard or landmark they can see by lantern or moonlight.

'Sail all the way to big land,' Wesley cries, holding his lantern high. He wants *Sea Devil* to take him further south – past the islands of the Torres Strait, past the pearling station on Waiben – and drop him off on the coloured sands of his homeland. 'Make spear. Go huntin'.'

The Thursday Island wharf is bustling with fishermen and traders, carts and cargo, and old men splicing ropes and mending nets, but it's the big mail steamer that catches Wesley's attention. He hurries over to the captain. 'Misser Cap'n. Goin' south? Want crew?'

The chubby man shakes his head and continues filling his pipe with tobacco. He is heading northwest, across the seas to Europe. 'No more coloured boys on this run,' he says, quoting from his new list of instructions. 'Only white men are permitted to transport mail from Australia.'

Wesley listens to him, puzzled. 'Blackfella not read letters.' Even if his mob could read, they wouldn't attempt to read Government mail. 'Hard words . . . Bible words.'

The captain strikes a match and lights his pipe. 'Officials fear that coloured carriers could put security at risk. A Post and Telegraph Act will be passed in parliament.' He sucks his pipe and considers the risk. 'Mail could get into the hands of the wrong people, I suppose. People of white race will be conducting the business of the new Commonwealth.' He turns and wanders off.

'Where you find all them whitefellas?' Wesley calls after the captain. 'Only black worker in Torres Strait.' But his words drift away unanswered.

He dawdles back to *Sea Devil* and helps the boys unload the catch. Back and forth they go, carrying heavy baskets and hessian sacks to the packing-shed, fending off hungry seabirds that shriek and dive at the smelly fish baskets. Greely's shells go in a pile to be counted and weighed and scrubbed clean for export.

The pearl-shell inspector follows the boys and examines the catch. He strokes his neat trimmed beard and grunts. 'Your skipper needs a stern reminder.' He marches off to find Greely.

'You are harvesting too many immature shells, Greely,' he cautions. 'You're depleting the resource and threatening oyster reproduction. Soon there will be no shell-beds left to harvest.'

'Pearlers have to make a living,' Greely argues. 'There's no size limit, no restrictions.'

'So you scoop up every small shell and make a quick profit with no regard to the future?' The inspector rocks back on the heels of his shiny black boots. 'How will that preserve the shell-grounds and benefit the industry?'

'Who cares about five years' time?' Greely snaps back. 'This season is what's important!'

'Over-fishing. Exploitation. How will shell-beds recuperate?'

Greely walks away; he doesn't care. He has a pump now, his diver can stay on the sea-floor for hours at a time. He'll raise a ton of shell. He'll make money while he can.

'Follow me, I have something to show you,' the inspector says, waving the boys to his office. They follow him obediently, curious. He opens a polished wooden box and shows them jewellery and other items inlaid with mother-of-pearl. Bracelets. Buckles. Powder boxes. Umbrella and cutlery handles, all shimmering with beautiful designs. 'This is top-quality mother-of-pearl,' he says, 'and it comes from the Torres Strait.' The boys stare wide-eyed, hands behind their backs, not daring to touch the pretty pieces. 'Any one of you boys could have harvested this shell.' He smiles and places the items carefully back in the velvet-lined box. 'Don't you feel proud of yourselves?' He dismisses them with a wave.

Sario is still beaming when they rush off to collect their pay. He's never seen such fine handwork, tiny delicate pieces of shell set in intricate patterns and pictures. How much would they cost? If he had money, he'd buy Apu the pretty hairbrush with the sea picture on the back. She'd love how the pearl-shell shimmers in the light when the brush is moved, how the silvery yacht appears to be sailing under a glossy moon.

It's almost five o'clock and the Shipping Office is due to close. The clerk shuffles through papers and rummages in the money safe. 'There is nothing here for you.'

No pay? Sario urges him to look again. 'I was to be paid on discharge in current coin.'

'I don't see your Agreement. Did any person witness your mark?'

Sario nods. 'A Manila-boy, a diver – we were both articled to Captain Greely's lugger, *Sea Devil*.'

'Fetch the boy.'

'I c-can't.' A lump rises in his throat. 'A shark took him.'

The clerk's eyebrows arch – is this lad trying to pull the wool over his eyes? 'How long did your vessel remain at sea?'

'Five d-days diving and extra days to load supplies and sail to and from . . . nine d . . .' Sario chokes on his words. Visions of his friend flash through his mind – the

Manila-boy here in this office, pushing him to sign the Agreement paper; the two of them flattening cockroaches and stocking the lugger with tinned food. His friend's blood colouring the water, the swirling red sea.

'You didn't work a full month, then?'

'We lost a d-diver and the weather turned b-bad. We had a good haul.' He wants the questions to stop. He wants his money. He wants to go home.

'You only dived five days and you expect a month's pay?'

The wall clock is ticking loudly. 'No.' Sario shakes his head. 'Just the money owed to me.' He'll take anything right now – a penny, even. He sags with hopelessness. The Manila-boy has gone, and no one can confirm he signed the Terms of Agreement paper.

The clerk notices Greely's cash book on the counter, the ledger he left with a loose sheet of paper. It isn't Sario's Agreement, it's his account, his bill. 'You spent your pay on luxuries from the slop-chest, you ran up an account with the captain.' His finger runs down the column of figures, the crew's pay and purchases. 'Nil to pay,' he says, showing Sario the deduction from his wage. 'Your pay just covers the luxury item you purchased.'

Luxury item? Sario stares wide-eyed at the clerk. He bought one shirt – a neat button-down shirt to farewell his Manila friend. He purchased nothing more from the slop-chest. No sweets. No biscuits.

'Sign here.' The man dips his pen in a bottle of ink. 'Your debt is paid. No pay to collect.'

Sario scrawls his name beside his purchase: *One buttoned shirt.* He can't argue, he did buy the shirt. No dispute.

He strides out the door and up the dirt road – long angry strides of frustration. One buttoned shirt couldn't cost nine days' pay! Greely is a crook! He's a cheat – he profits from the slop-chest.

What will he tell Apu?

Sario hurries past the public houses and sickening smells of strong liquor. The hotels are noisy places at sundown, after boat crews collect their pay – loud arguments, unruly fistfights, rowdy singers and plonking pianos.

But he finds home too quiet. Too still. No wheezing. No coughing. No pounding of herbs. No fire crackling in the cooking stones. He rushes to the vegetable garden, but only the fowls are there to greet him, flapping and clucking with surprise.

'Your apu is in the hospital,' a boy calls to him. 'Two days.'

Sario runs to the doctor's place and bursts through the doors, his heart pounding. His ill mother is lying on the high white bed, perspiring and frail, skin and bone, strung out like seaweed. Sario can't speak, he's numb; his apu should be well by now.

Leilani puts aside her water bowl and washcloth and props Apu up with pillows. 'She needs stronger medicine, now.' She mouths the words. 'Will your pay cover the cost?'

Medicine. Lung treatment. He'll be sinking in debt again. And no pay! How much could he get for the tiny pearl?

The doctor appears with a hard rubber pipe and a small bottle of liquid. 'Clamp this pipe between your lips,' he instructs Apu. 'Take ten deep inhalations. This should reach the deepest part of your respiratory tract. There should be no need to cough or gag.'

Leilani takes Sario aside and shows him a row of medicine jars on Apu's bedside cabinet. The labels say they are bronchial formulas prepared by specialists in London. Sario can read the price – two shillings and sixpence a jar. Leilani picks up a small corked bottle. 'This syrup is more expensive and Apu has three doses a day.' The bottle is almost empty. What can he say?

Monsoon rain is pelting the shack that evening, loosening boards and blowing through cracks, when he breaks the sad news to Leilani. Sario explains with gestures how he waved and shouted to the Manila-boy to warn him about the shark. How the cruel Japee pushed him under and forced him to dive with the shark. 'He was a kind Manila-boy,' Sario cries. 'He only wanted to go back home to his family – blackbirders kidnapped him from his village.' He continues, explaining about the slop-chest, how he purchased a shirt to farewell his friend and Greely kept all his money. Nine days' pay for one shirt! 'How much does a shirt cost?'

Leilani rolls her eyes. How would she know? Store clothes are luxuries she can't afford. She sews their few clothes, stitching by candlelight late into the night, the way the missionaries taught her. How will they manage now? She already owes money to the store. She buries her head in her hands. Sario should not have spent the money, but she understands his reason.

She takes out her pounding stone and mixing bowl. Why do those wicked men – Hiroshi and the captain – take advantage of hardworking young boys? The storm rages and so does her fury.

Sario unties the knot in the corner of his blanket and shows Leilani the precious little pearl. 'I sell pearl. Pay for medicine.'

She rolls the creamy pearl in the palm of her hand and wishes she could keep it. It's dented. Misshapen. 'How much money you get?'

He looks blank. He knows nothing about pearls or their value. 'I get good price,' he says. He has to.

The next morning Sario approaches a tall Indian man in Douglas Street near the Metropole Hotel. The trader looks respectable, neatly dressed in a white turban and a long white shirt that billows over his loose cotton trousers.

'It's a baroque pearl.' He rolls the little pearl between the tips of his manicured fingers. 'Not perfectly round, of lesser value.' He looks Sario up and down, his dark eyes assessing the island boy. 'There could be flaws . . . I will examine it with my eyeglass and we'll discuss price on Monday. Meet me here.'

Sario beams, in awe of the tall man. He's experienced and knowledgeable and yarns like a gentleman.

He spots the pearl-trader again the following morning, striding down the road in his towering turban. He waves to the man as he and Leilani enter the church. 'Pray that he pays a good price,' he gestures to her. 'Pray for Apu.'

After church, Sario wanders the foreshore, the cool, fresh breeze leaving a salty taste on his tongue. He sits under the wongai tree feeling blessed and at peace – his mother's breathing is much better now, and money is coming from the Indian trader to pay the bills.

The seabirds peck and claw at a broken branch lying in the sandy soil. Sario can see the shape of a dolphin in the hard, grainy wood, and takes out the small knife the elders gave him. He'll define the shape and smooth the lines and surprise Apu with a gift. The wongai leaves are round, and the fruit is small and fleshy, but the plums are not ripe yet.

Wesley comes and plonks down beside Sario. 'Eat plum when ripe, brudda.' He wouldn't eat the fruit himself – he doesn't want to keep returning here. He knows the old legend: *Eat the fruit of the wongai tree – ensure you return to TI.*

Chapter Twenty-Two

Leilani is busy chopping and mixing strange smelling herbs when Sario leaves the beach shack to find the pearl-trader and collect his money. Wesley helps him search the streets and stores and public houses, even the Post Office, but the Indian trader is nowhere about.

Wesley points to a crowd gathering at the end of the long jetty. 'Go packing shed, brudda.' They can see Greely and other pearlers moving inside, the steamy heat driving them to shelter under its iron roof. The boys follow – the Indian trader could be there.

The pearl-shell inspector opens the meeting. 'Coloured men will not be permitted to work on boats after Federation,' he says. 'White Australia will be the new rule.'

His words are bait drawing them to debate. They roar in protest. 'How do we pay white man's wages and make a profit? Coloured labour is cheap, it's affordable.'

Greely bellows from the back. 'Allowances will have to be made for pearl-shell fishing. We are a specialist industry.'

The others agree. 'We support a white Australia, of course we do,' one skipper says. 'But pearl-shelling is undesirable work – white men can't be expected to do it. The hours are long and living space is cramped. Diving is difficult and dangerous.'

'And where do we find all these white men?' another skipper roars. 'White workers are scarce in the islands and most of them lack experience. They demand such high wages we couldn't make a profit even if we had the workers!'

'It would take months to teach them the skills, diving and shelling and tendering,' Greely shouts. 'The costs would ruin us.'

The inspector nods; it is true, there would be a labour shortage. Most white divers have left the islands already, unhappy with the risks, the low wages and the dwindling shell-beds.

'Japanese are hard-working and profitable, they could provide a large labour force. Why can't they stay?'

'Japanese contribute little to our country's wealth,' the inspector snaps. 'They import food from Japan, buy goods from Japanese shops, and send their wages back to Japan!' He mops his face with a handkerchief. 'Some divers send home a hundred yen a year, which is a lot of money in Japan. The wage in Japan is around forty yen.'

He gulps down a full glass of water. 'Pearl divers support families and sometimes whole villages, they educate children and purchase farms. This is admirable, but it doesn't benefit Australia's economy.'

He fills his glass again and continues. 'There are more Japanese in Torres Strait than white men.' He looks forward to the new Immigration Restriction Act when they'll all be excluded from the country. 'Asians are getting a foothold in the industry, they're building more boats and they're industrious workers, they could squeeze you all out,' he says. 'And they pose a defence risk.'

'All work boats should be owned by British subjects!' Greely announces. 'Our government should forbid Asian ownership.'

The skippers nod and mutter among themselves. They agree, but still they face a dilemma. 'White men don't want to do the dangerous work and mainland blacks don't want to stay and work. What do we do?'

'Binghis have a good knowledge of the sea, but they'll abscond if they can,' Greely adds.

'Who could blame them?' the inspector replies. 'Aborigines are often treated badly and given little incentive to work. Children as young as six are kidnapped and forced to dive, it's a disgrace. Some have been left stranded on outer islands.'

'Binghis are better off at sea with us,' another skipper pipes up. 'They hunt for shells and get tucker provided, they're well fed. It's better than roaming the scrub.'

'We blackfellas, we cheap workers,' Wesley whispers to Sario, as they look around the packing shed for the pearl-trader. The tall Indian with the turban is nowhere to be seen.

The pearl-shell inspector packs up his notes and concludes, 'There will be many more discussions before Federation.'

'Pearling crews will never be *all* white.' Greely winks at the boys as they go out the door. 'White Australia or not!'

Sario stops a boy pulling a handcart along the jetty. 'You see a tall Indian man? White turban?'

'White suit?'

'Yes.' Sario nods, encouraging the boy to talk more.

'He left on steamer at sun-up, high tide.' The boy heard the Indian arguing the price of his ticket – eight pounds to Brisbane steerage class. 'Paid his passage with pearls.'

Sario stumbles away, a bad taste in his mouth, more bitter than bilge water. He was a fool to trust the trader with his pearl. He didn't even ask the Indian his name!

Leilani arrives home after sundown, dripping wet and still angry with Greely and Hiroshi for their bad behaviour. She shakes off the rainwater and rubs herself down with a cloth. She spots Sario huddled in a corner and hurries to him. 'Something wrong, *babat*?'

'I was a fool to trust the pearl-trader,' Sario sobs. Leilani lights a candle to see his hand gestures as he tells her the whole story: how he searched everywhere for the Indian trader, how the man stole their pearl and bought a ticket for the steamship. Now he can't buy medicine for Apu. 'No pay . . . no pearl . . . nothing.'

'Sshh.' Leilani rocks Sario gently, her voice soothing, calming him. 'I have a little money,' she whispers. 'Should pay the bills.' She goes to the corner where she keeps her mixing bowl and takes out a small woven basket. She tips it up and coins roll out over the woven mat.

Sario gathers the coins, his hands trembling. 'Where you get this?'

She grins. 'Sell taro, eggs, balm.' Her garden is thriving with the wet season rain. 'You see taro? *Dawa?*' She grows healthy taro and bananas, more than enough, and pump-divers pay well for her soothing balm, it eases their sore muscles. 'Clever healer!'

Sario relaxes. 'You wise *ngoka*.' His sister is smart; he needn't worry about going back to sea and leaving the deaf girl to care for her sick mother. Leilani can handle anything. He's the burden of the family. He's the fool who was easily cheated, who lost his pearl and his pay. They could do without him!

But he couldn't live without them, his kin. He takes Leilani's hands in his. 'I sail to Erub at sun-up.' The Darnley Deeps are far away and he'll be gone a long time. She'll have to take care of everything.

She nods and scoops up the coins. 'You bring home pay, *babat*,' she warns. This is all the money she has, and it will just pay the bills.

Sario heads to the jetty before sun-up, leaving Leilani sleeping. A southerly wind is blowing, *Sea Devil* is loaded and ready to sail, water and food provisions stowed and the dinghy lashed down. All crew are aboard – except two. 'Cap'n missin'. Pump-diver missin',' Wesley says, nibbling his lip with concern.

Sario scales back up the ladder to look for them. He sees Leilani running along the jetty in her new cotton dress, her pearl-shell necklace glinting in the dawn light.

'What are you doing here? Is it Apu?' He won't go to sea if his mother is worse. But he signed the Agreement paper for a ninety-day term! And they need the money!

'No. Bring these.' Leilani hands him a basket of cockroach baits and his shirt, freshly washed. She steps back into the shadows. 'No slop-chest,' she warns.

She's looking past him, over his shoulder, and suddenly stiffens. He spins around, following her worried gaze. 'Greely!'

Two boys are dragging the captain along the jetty, trying to carry him, but stumbling under his weight. Hiroshi is coming behind in the same unconscious state. What is wrong with them – are they drunk? Or worse?

He turns on Leilani. 'You did this? Gave them a strange potion?' His heart drums with fear. What has she done?

Leilani is puzzled – why is he angry with her? She strains to hear his words.

Sario shakes her to answer. 'They could die! What was in your concoction? *Upiri?* Poison?' What if the captain and diver don't wake up? How will he work? Earn money?

She shakes her head, wide-eyed.

'They die – *you* go prison.' Sario stabs her chest with his finger. 'You meddle with dangerous *lukup*, Leilani.'

Tears of frustration fill her eyes. Unfair! He's got it all wrong. 'No, *babat*!'

Greely's carriers dump him on a bunk and disappear into the dawn. The two boys carrying Hiroshi trip on a plank and lose their balance. They drop the Japee. He slides down the metal ladder and hits the deck. *Crack!* Hiroshi's knee strikes a barrel of water filled to the brim, but he doesn't move or make a sound. The boys flee.

The Kanaka takes the wheel. 'Toss the ropes!' he shouts.

Sario turns away from Leilani, casts off the mooring ropes and scrambles down the ladder. He feels the men's necks for a pulse – both are breathing, at least. Leilani's sleeping drug wouldn't kill them . . . would it? How much did she give them? A pinch? A spoonful? More? He glares up at her on the jetty, placing his hands together. 'Pray they both wake up!' he mouths.

Leilani shrugs. The men are drunk, that's all. They must be. She saw them drinking on the hotel veranda at sundown, Greely forcing the Japee to drink more alcohol, to be his drinking mate, to keep his job. They'll sleep it off, and Sario and the crew will have some peace.

Sea Devil catches the breeze and glides over the waves as graceful as a manta ray, her sails set. Wesley watches the fiery sun break over the horizon, and the clouds and sky turn red. 'Red sky in the mornin', sailor take warnin',' he cautions.

The crew ignore him.

The Kanaka outlines their dive plans as they sail. 'If the harvest is good, we'll stay six or seven weeks on the shell-beds. A mother-ship will come by and collect our catch and bring fresh supplies.'

Chapter Twenty-Three

Sea Devil finally reaches the Darnley Deeps, and the boys drop anchor, the chain rattling a long way to the bottom. They see the shallow reefs way off in the distance. 'Swimming-divers will be rowing a long way,' Cook says.

The Kanaka hurries Hiroshi into his heavy canvas suit. 'Dive conditions are perfect,' he says, strapping on the heavy lead boots and bolting down the helmet. He helps Hiroshi onto the ladder, shuts the face-glass and watches him drop below the surface.

Sario tidies the decks and plants the last of the cockroach baits. He peers over the side, watching and waiting for a shell bag to come up. How long has it been?

The tender is growing restless. There's nothing coming up the rope. No shells. No messages. The sea is calm, the water clear, why isn't the Japee finding shell? Are they on a bad patch?

He shakes the lifeline rope. *All right?* 'If the diver doesn't send up a shell bag soon, we'll have to raise the anchor and drag him across the shell-bed.'

Another five minutes and no signal. Is he in trouble down there?

He feels tugs on the rope. *Four ... five ... six ... urgent!* Seven tugs! Danger!

The tender draws the rope slowly to the surface, but he can feel the Japee is rising too quickly, scrambling up hand over hand. The Kanaka shakes his head. 'This bad, this bad!' He's learnt never to rush a diver's ascent, no matter the danger – staging a rise from the very deep is critical.

Hiroshi surfaces and the tender quickly unscrews his helmet. Sario helps him haul Hiroshi aboard. The Japee's eyes stare back, wide and terror-stricken, his face as white as sun-bleached coral. 'Ghost!' he shrieks. 'Came out of the blue.'

The pump-boys rush to help pull off his suit, but Hiroshi rubs his knee and howls with pain. 'Paralyse!' he screams, and curls into a ball on the deck. He will *not* go down again.

The Japee's howling and shrieking spooks the whole crew. The pump-boys circle him at a distance. 'He's mad!' they cry. 'Gone crackers!'

'If he doesn't go down again soon, we won't get paid,' Cook complains.

The Kanaka scans the ocean and the islands off in the distance. 'Shallow reefs are a long row from here,' he says. 'It's too late in the day to send the swimming-divers out.' He scratches his stubbly beard and wonders what to do. Should he up anchor and move to shallower waters and give the swimming-divers an early start in the morning? Or will Hiroshi come to his senses and dive the Darnley Deeps?

'Send Sario down,' Cook suggests. 'He's experienced in these waters.'

'No!' Sario backs away, shaking his head. He doesn't know how to use a pump, no one has shown him. He's never dived this deep!

'It's your chance, Sario.' Cook smiles encouragement. 'It's your dream.'

He should be excited, but he's a bundle of fear. Darnley Deeps is a dangerous place. Everyone knows many divers die down there!

'Try-dive first,' the Kanaka says in a no-nonsense voice. 'I'll talk you through it, an hour down at a time.'

Sario hangs back, his insides twisting like an eel up a spear.

'Phantom!' Hiroshi cries out. 'Came at me . . . out of the blue.' He crawls to the cabin door and cowers by the step.

'Look at the Japee!' Sario shrieks. 'That's what Darnley Deeps does to a diver!' He signed on *Sea Devil* to learn to pump-dive, not to become a raving lunatic! He clings to the boat gunnel and turns to Wesley to back him up. But the binghi is terror-stricken as well, staring at the Japee as if Hiroshi were a ghost himself.

Is it the deep that sent Hiroshi crazy, or Leilani's potion? It has to be the deep. He's seen divers like this wandering the Waiben village – damaged men, babbling to themselves, their bodies crippled and minds gone.

Cook passes off the Japee's odd behaviour. 'Hiroshi's imagination is running wild, that's all. It's lonely at the bottom.'

The Kanaka drops the lead-line over the side and Sario watches the marker tags disappear . . . *ten* . . . *twenty* . . . 'It's thirty fathoms deep!' he cries. He's been down to eight fathoms, and that was scary – swimming divers only have one breath. Even with an air-pipe, he'd be terrified to go thirty fathoms deep! Any diver would.

Hiroshi clutches his knee and writhes on the deck, his face pale and twisting with pain. The pump-boys battle to get him unbuckled and out of his suit.

Cook plies the diver with whisky. 'Sip this, it will numb your pain.' He holds a mug to Hiroshi's lips and studies his sore knee. It's the same knee he cracked when he slid down the jetty ladder and struck the water barrel.

'There's not a mark to be seen,' Cook says, extremely puzzled.

Sario slumps to the deck and wraps his arms tightly around his body. Did the Jap really see monsters down in the deep?

Greely staggers from his cabin, gruff and groggy. 'What's wrong with him?' he grunts, stepping over Hiroshi and scanning the sea. 'It's flat calm – why isn't he down?' He turns and bellows at the tender, 'Get a diver in the water!'

'You're our best diver, Sario,' Cook pleads. He's watched this quick young diver from Torres Strait. 'No one has your experience.'

Sario slinks away. He slips down through the hatch and crawls deep into the boat's framework, into *Sea Devil*'s underbelly. He huddles there among her ribs, sick with fear, a musty smell of mildew all around.

Wesley follows. 'Don't go down, brudda.' The whites of his eyes flash a warning in the dark. 'Big mudda ghost live in the deep. Catch you. Run away.'

They hear Greely's voice come booming through the hatch. 'Get dressed, Sario. You're going down.'

'I c-can't d-dive with a pump.'

'Time to learn!'

'It's thirty f-fathoms deep!'

'Take short dips first,' Greely instructs. 'Every diver has to start somewhere.' He turns to Cook. 'Get in the hold and fetch that boy.'

Cook drags him out. 'No pearl-shell, no money, Sario. You can do it.' He forces him up through the hatch. 'Think of your mother, she needs treatment and hospital care.'

Greely slaps Sario about the ears. 'Stop wasting my time!'

'I don't know how to p-pump-d-dive,' Sario cries. 'I don't know how to breathe with an air-pipe.'

'Get down and learn!'

Sario watches the tender lay out the air-pipes and polish the copper diving helmet and clean the thick face-glass. His belly churns. He lurches over to the side and vomits into the ocean.

'It's strange at first, but you'll settle down after a while.' The tender hands him the diving vest and cap. 'Don't worry, air will pump into your helmet constantly. All you have to do is breathe.'

Sario reels back from the stink of garlic and ginger – the flannel diving vest and woollen cap reek of the Japee, even the canvas diving-suit. The tender buckles the leather straps and sits the heavy metal corselet over Sario's shoulders. He buckles up the lead boots and tightens the rubber wrist bands. He fastens a lanyard and knife to his belt.

Sario can barely move under the weight. The lead boots are heavy and impossible to lift. The tender shuffles him to the ladder. 'Take a short dip first.' He bolts the helmet into the brass corselet, screwing it down to seal it and make it watertight. He ties a lifeline rope around Sario's waist and helps him over the side and onto the rope ladder. 'Feel the valve at the side of the helmet? Turn it right to close off the air or left to open the holes.' He screws the face-glass shut.

Sario panics. What if he forgets which way to turn? He's trussed up like a fowl roasting in this suit, and his life is in the hands of two young pump-boys!

'Make your signals clear.' The tender repeats instructions through the face-glass. '*Two pulls for more air.*

Four pulls to haul up. Seven pulls for danger. Shake the rope for all right.'

Sario can read his lips, he's practised with Leilani . . . but what if he forgets the code? He feels for the air valve and prays.

'Stay down an hour or so, this is just a try-dive. You won't go to the bottom today.'

That's for certain! Sario nods back.

The tender shouts down to the pump-boys. 'Pump away!'

Sario clings to the rope ladder, nervous but excited. Air hisses in through the back of his helmet and his suit inflates, a strange, eerie feeling.

The rope ladder is short – the last rung hangs just a few feet below the surface of the water. Where is the bottom step? He can't feel it in his thick boots. He can't see it; the big helmet is fixed and won't move. He tugs his lifeline rope. He's encased in a coffin!

The tender taps on his face-glass and waves him off. 'Go!'

Sario takes a deep breath, it's habit, but he doesn't need to – air is flowing in. He separates his lifeline rope from his air-pipe and steps off.

He floats a little and then descends, as fat and full as a dugong.

Air blows down in front of his face, an eerie whistling sound, frightening yet exhilarating. It's a strange sensation. No need to hold his breath. Bubbles rise. He can look around and take his time. The ocean is warm and sunlit and clouds of fish swim by. A large green turtle flaps down beside him, crusty barnacles stuck to its shell.

The pressure of the water increases. Sario clings to his lifeline rope and checks that his air-pipe is paying out behind him. '*Not too tight to restrict its movement,*' the tender warned. '*Not too slack to allow it to drag and snag.*'

He goes deeper. The water grows colder, but it's clearer. He can see ahead the length of a canoe – even further. The broad wings of a manta ray. A giant groper. Pink jellyfish pulsing along. The suit is buoyant and he feels more confident; the weight is lightening somehow.

The pressure of the water closes in. It's sudden. His head thumps. His ears hurt as if spears are pressing into his eardrums. Short breaths. *Pull. Pull. Pull. Pull.* The pressure increases – more than he can bear. *Pull. Pull. Pull.* He scales the rope to rise faster. Blood splatters his face-glass.

The tender unscrews his helmet. 'Don't come up that fast again!' he bellows. 'Stage your ascent.'

Sario spits blood, unblocking his ears and nose. The tender helps him out of the suit and warns, 'Rise gradually from the deep, it's important. Divers' disease claims many lives.' He doesn't know why it's so, but rising slowly relieves pressure. He's seen divers surface quickly, screaming in pain, their joints out of shape, knees and elbows crippling. 'Darnley Deeps is a divers' graveyard. Some never come up.'

Wesley steers Sario to the back of the boat and spreads his thin blanket on the deck. 'Rest, brudda.'

Hiroshi is still howling and rubbing his knee. Did he come up too fast? Old divers say the pain is worse where there's injury.

Sario nestles in his blanket and massages his drumming ears . . . Pump-diving isn't what he expected.

Chapter Twenty-Four

Fine weather, a slack morning tide. Sario shuffles across the deck in the heavy diving boots and swings onto the ladder. The dive-suit is snug and familiar now, his smell penetrating the canvas. He will conquer his fears this time. He might even go to the bottom and haul up a load of shell.

Hiroshi watches. He doesn't want this quick young diver taking his job, taking his money, but he's afraid and in pain, his knee bent out of shape. Will the island boy see ghosts when he goes down deep? Cook tells him he's crazy, that the ghosts are in his head. But are they? They seem real. Hiroshi's scared to dive deep again.

Wesley frowns with worry as Sario straightens his lifeline. 'Deep, brudda.'

The tender screws the helmet down, attaches a lanyard and knife to Sario's belt, and hooks a shell-bag to his corselet. 'Remember to rise slowly and stage your ascent.'

He screws Sario's face-glass tight and signals the pump-hands to turn the wheels. 'Pump away!'

Air whistles in through the brass pipe at the back of the helmet and the suit inflates. *Splash!* Sario sees *Sea Devil*'s copper keel glinting as he descends, his air-pipe and lifeline paying out rapidly. Deeper. Colder. The pressure builds in his ears. How far to the bottom? His heart thumps, his stomach churns. Should he go all the way? His eyes adjust to the fairyland around him. Orange striped fish . . . silver trevally and brown spotted cod . . . brilliant sea-flowers, yellow and green . . . soft golden corals waving with the current. Everything is big – magnified in the watery deep. Monster sea fans. Giant clams with spotted lips. Squid the size of groper.

His ears pop. The pain stops. He hits the bottom . . . *thud!*

Pink coral rocks. Vivid blue sea-stars. Pearl-shells buried in the sand, their ruffled edges poking up, just visible. They're awkward to pick up in the cumbersome suit, and they're scarcer than he'd imagined.

Stoop to scoop the shells, the tender warned. *Don't bend over, your helmet could take in water.*

Sario bounces along with the tide, spidery crabs scuttling out of his way. He has to swing his whole body to scan the sea-floor, his helmet fixed and screwed down tight. A shell here. A shell there. Sea-slugs burrowing in the sand.

A sudden jerk on the rope. *All right?*

All right! He shakes back, confident now, much calmer with his breathing settled. He's filled his shell-bag twice already, and sent up ten to twelve shells at a time. He's doing well.

The sunlight suddenly dims. A message comes on the rope – seven tugs. *Ascend! Danger!*

Sario looks up. A dark shadow. *Shark!* His heart races, his throat goes dry. The shark is twice his size – long and smooth. *Stay on the bottom and wait till a shark moves on,* the Kanaka warned.

But the monster isn't leaving; it's circling between him and the lugger. Who can help? No one – he's too far down for swimming divers. If he goes up, he'll be mauled to death. If he stays down, same ending. Sario feels for the knife, his temper boiling. He'll stab the shark. He'll kill it before it kills him.

Bubbles will sometimes scare off a shark. Lift your helmet slightly to release them.

What if his bubbles anger the shark? What if it tangles in his rope and pulls out his air-pipe? No choice! He lifts his helmet and watches the bubbles rise, his heart thumping under his canvas suit.

The shark goes! Swims off. *Haul up! Tug. Tug. Tug. Tug!*

Sario rises slowly, cautious, alert, the knife gripped tight in his right hand. He releases more bubbles as he goes, unsure of the shark's position and still a long way from the top.

Wesley smiles as he breaks the surface. 'Big-fella shark. Him run away.' He unhooks Sario's shell-basket and hands him a mug of hot tea.

Greely isn't happy with the small haul; only a few dozen shells are lying on the deck. 'Comb the patch again,' he barks.

'But the shark is still down there!'

'It's gone!' Greely sets the lugger's sail for another sweep of the reef and *Sea Devil* beats windward, drifting with speed.

Down on the seabed Sario has to run to keep up, his heavy boots scraping the muddy bottom, his eyes adjusting to the dim light, his head pounding. He scours the sea floor as best he can, bouncing and buffeting along in the current, scooping every shell he sees. He fills his canvas bag over and over, attaching it to the rope and signalling the tender. *Bag full. Haul up.*

Later in the day the sea turns murky and a strong tide drags him over the rough coral. His bag is full and he's cold, tired and hungry. *Tug! Tug! Come up! Come up!*

A sudden jerk brings him to a stop halfway. He looks back. His air-pipe is snagged on coral. He swims back down to release it, but it's wedged tight. He wriggles and tugs, but the rubbery pipe won't budge. He slows his breathing; his pipe is crushed and less air can filter in. The pipe is snagged again, just above, stretched tight between the two coral bommies and grinding away on a hard coral plate! *Tug. Tug. Tug. Tug. Tug. Danger! Help!*

No response. His pipe will snap and cut off his air! Where is his tender? No reply . . . no signal at all. His rope is limp. Why is the tender so slow? *Tug. Tug. Tug. Tug. Tug. Tug! Danger!*

'*Keep a clear head at all times. Presence of mind could save your life.*'

What can he do? *Pull. Pull. Pull. Pull. Pull. Pull. Pull.* His air will soon be gone!

No one is coming. He's thirty fathoms down! He'll die in this watery grave!

He feels a sea-snake coil up his leg. He yanks it and tries to pull it off, but it won't release, won't uncoil. He snatches up his knife and lashes out. Its head sways, taunting him. He's angry, he slashes again. It wriggles and falls – he's sliced it in two.

That's what he has to do – slash his air-pipe the same way. Cut it, before it wears through.

He opens the valve to inflate his suit. A little air filters in through the crushed pipe. Is it enough to get him to the surface? He screws the valve shut, locking the air in, and slows his breathing even more.

The rubbery pipe is tough to cut. He needs more air, more strength to saw through it. His arms are heavy and weak, his head dizzy.

Snap! He's cut through! He's rising. Scared. Short of breath. No hissing sound, no air coming in. Lightheaded.

Air! Air! He waves for the helmet to come off. He sucks air deep into his lungs.

He sees the Japee holding his rope. 'Why does *he* have my lifeline?'

'Hiroshi is learning to tender,' the Kanaka says, smiling with relief and help Sario onto the lugger.

'Not with my life!' Sario snatches his rope from Hiroshi. 'He didn't respond to my signal! I could be dead! Snagged on the coral.'

'There was nothing we could do, Sario.' The Kanaka examines the sawn-off length of rubbery pipe hanging from his helmet. 'You cut your air-pipe and saved your own life. It was the only thing you could do.'

Chapter Twenty-Five

The waves are steep, the sea riled up by a strong running tide, white foam flying. 'The Strait is bearing the push and pull of two powerful seas, the Coral Sea and Arafura Sea,' Greely says. 'Go do your dip, boy. Your new pipe is set to go.'

Sario backs away, more fearful now that something will go wrong. His pipe could snag again! His rope could tangle! Terrible dangers could strike him down in the deep. 'Not today.'

'Come on.' The Kanaka steps forward with the dive-suit to reassure him. 'I will be your tender today.'

'No shell. No money,' Cook urges.

Sario's thoughts go to Apu, struggling for breath, trying to clear her lungs. Her health rests on his shoulders – if he doesn't earn money how will he keep paying for her treatment and get her well again? He dresses slowly and goes down.

The pressure of the water increases, squeezing air from his lungs. He crawls along the muddy bottom, feeling his way, nervous. The shell-bed is thin and patchy, well worked-over by previous divers, and visibility is poor, dark and gloomy. He doesn't feel well . . . foggy. *Tug. Tug. Tug. Tug.* He's only collected three shells, but he is going up.

Pain strikes. It's more intense as he rises. His elbows and knees are on fire, his shoulders pierced with burning spears. His ears buzz, his mind wanders. Then coldness. A deep, sudden chill seeps into his lungs. He's losing track . . . losing consciousness.

The tender draws him to the surface, a limp weight on his rope. But still he stages the diver's rise – five minutes' pause at fifteen feet – ten minutes at ten feet. Sario rallies. The rope is taut and he is swinging, dazed. He pauses again at five feet – twenty minutes more in the bone-chilling cold.

He tries to speak when the helmet comes off, but his tongue lolls about in his mouth, unable to form words. A sudden spasm grips him – a seizure. He collapses. The tender undresses him, removing his weights and corselet, unbuckling his boots and suit.

Sario's skin is blotchy and purple with rash. Wesley drags him to the aft deck, to his blanket. He warms a pan of oil over the fire and massages Sario's arms and legs. 'Water too deep, brudda,' he says. 'Killum you inside.' He kneads Sario's joints, his long bony fingers pressing deeply, breaking down knots of tight muscle, straightening bent limbs.

Sario can barely hear the binghi above the racket. The crew are yelling instructions and tossing ropes to a large schooner manoeuvring alongside, her mainsail holding her into the brisk south-easterly. Both crews are hitching and securing lines.

The tall, wiry captain steps aboard. He studies *Sea Devil*'s catch, his eyebrows arching with surprise. 'Is this your whole harvest?' His mother-ship picks up catches and delivers supplies, allowing smaller boats to stay longer on the shell-beds. 'Yours is the worst catch by far.'

He notices Sario curled up and shivering in his blanket. 'Get yourself a decent diver, Greely. You should be harvesting sixty to a hundred shell-pairs a day.' He looks around at the crew. 'Japanese are good divers, they seem to have a knack for finding shell buried in mud.'

Sario pulls the small blanket up over his head. He's a hopeless pump-diver, scared stiff and sore all over. The Japee can have the job, he won't fight him for it.

He cries through the night with his pain and shame, and worries how he'll support his mother and sister and help his clan now.

The Kanaka is restless as well, up and down and in and out of his cabin, one eye on Sario and the other on the night sky. 'Big change coming . . . bad weather.'

Chapter Twenty-Six

Sea Devil is flying south when Sario crawls from his blanket, strong winds pushing her towards the mainland and more fertile shell-grounds.

Wesley jigs with excitement. 'Goin' south, brudda. Goin' home!'

Hiroshi sits on the roof of the cabin, legs crossed, watching the boys. He catches Sario's eye and nods, as if giving his approval.

For what? Sario looks away, an empty feeling in his gut. The Japee won the battle and kept the job, and now he's gloating. He won't fight him for the work, he's powerless now; he'll accept defeat and let his dream go. Pump-diving is scary anyway . . . and painful.

Hiroshi limps down from the cabin roof and sits beside Sario. 'I feel your pain,' he says. 'I suffer divers' disease also.' He massages his knee, the knee he cracked when he hit the water barrel.

Sario ignores him.

'I apologise,' Hiroshi says. 'I should not be angry with you. You good diver, and you help haul me up and get me on board.'

Sario turns his back, outraged. It's too late for apologies and compliments! The Japee pushed his friend down with a shark and killed him! He busted his ribs in the packing shed and smashed his toes with a kero drum. He stole his pearl-meat. And he left him to die, snagged on the coral!

Sea Devil is beating through the shipping channel, past the tip of mainland Cape York, past lush green trees and mountains fresh with wet-season rain. Gulls and terns are hovering above in the warm thermals, heads down, wings outstretched.

Hiroshi keeps apologising, explaining his bad behaviour and demanding Sario's attention. 'I need to earn money. I pump-dive to pay back big debt in Japan, support poor village and family.'

'I support my family too!' Sario snaps. 'Every diver needs money. Every diver works hard! My mother is ill, she has expensive medicine and treatment.'

The Japee earns forty shillings a month. And a portion of the catch – a further twenty pounds! He should share it with all the divers!

'If debt not paid I bring great shame and dishonour to my family.' Hiroshi lowers his eyes. He continues, telling Sario of his family's grinding poverty, of the elderly villagers who depend on his pay, and his strict Japanese culture. 'Great hardship,' he mutters. 'I sorry I behave badly. I am afraid to return home poor.'

He expects forgiveness and understanding? Sario boils with anger. 'You don't have to be cruel to prove your self-worth. There's no excuse for bad behaviour.'

Hiroshi hangs his head and sobs, admitting he is jealous of Sario's ability. 'Please forgive me?'

He *is* genuinely sorry, Sario realises. Japan must be a very different island to his Torres Strait *kaiwa*. His clan sing and laugh and enjoy themselves, they're happy souls, despite some bad treatment from a few white men.

'Australia big land,' Hiroshi says. 'Good opportunity to work and make money.' He nods. 'Head diver important man in Japan.' If Sario took his job, his good fortune would go and his reputation would be ruined.

Sario listens and understands. It would be difficult for Hiroshi to return home and shame his family, go back to peddling noodles on the street. He is ambitious for his future and wants to rise out of poverty.

Hiroshi smiles. 'Sunny days, warm seas, good conditions here.' Australia gave him confidence, offering him a comfortable life and a prosperous future, but he worries; he hasn't dived for three days, he hasn't earned a penny. And Sario is strong competition, a good diver, a quick swimmer.

Sario feels happier now that Hiroshi has apologised and explained his fears and bad behaviour. He tells

Wesley, 'Hiroshi supports his village and family in Japan. He has big debt to pay back.'

'Every fella has problems,' Wesley says. 'We all bruddas. We all bleed.'

Sario nods. 'Japees are not bad people; they work hard, and they don't give up without a fight.' He whistles as he thinks. Japanese people have brought good work ethics and some sensible ideas to the Torres Strait Islands – except for the stinking garlic and ginger!

'Careful,' Wesley warns, as the wind picks up and the sea turns dark and menacing. 'You whistle up storm, brudda!'

Chapter Twenty-Seven

All vessels are making for shelter, white sails dotting the angry black ocean – all skippers alert. 'Weather's getting worse,' Greely shouts, as *Sea Devil* pitches and tosses in the treacherous sea. Huge waves lift her high on foaming crests, then drop away to shuddering thuds. Strong winds scream through her rigging.

Wesley watches the dark clouds gather and build. 'Big-fella storm come.' He aches to sail further south – past Cape Melville and home to his mob – but this storm is impassable. Great flashes and crackles of electricity pierce the inky sky and bounce off the rocks along the coast. He huddles with the other boys for warmth and comfort.

Sea Devil turns into Bathurst Bay and they jostle with other craft for mooring space. A loud burst of lightning lights up the tall granite hills and the bare masts of schooners and luggers and other vessels seeking shelter. Is that the trader's sleek lugger he can see? Sario looks for the high cabin, but he can't be sure; the rain is heavy and the boats are rocking. Is Thaati sheltering here? Naku and Kadub?

Greely points her nose into the wind and they fasten her there, two anchors down to stop her drifting. 'Batten down!' he roars.

Sea Devil swings erratically on her long chains, rocking violently. The boys furl her sodden sails and clear the decks as quickly as they can, stinging rain blasting their skinny bodies and the wind whipping off with their breath. Loose items are flying and lamps are swaying.

Barometer needles drop and the air turns bone-chillingly cold. The wind howls and shrieks and spirals into hurricane intensity. Wild surf crashes onto the reef and thunders over the sand. Anchors drag. Boats crash. Masts snap and glass smashes. The noise is deafening, frightening.

Sario and the boys crawl down into the dark creaking bowels of the hull, seeking warmth and safety, their bodies wet and shivering. But nowhere is safe, no surface soft or comforting – it's just hard wooden frames and the savage storm raging.

All night they are tossed against the hard timbers. Bashing and crashing. Scared and cold. Their bodies bruised and bleeding. Sario howls for the storm to show mercy, for the wild, shrieking winds to stop. He howls for protection . . . for Apu and Leilani . . . for Thaati . . . for his clan. All Islanders will be suffering, the hurricane's so intense.

At dawn the air stills – a lull, the eye of the storm passing over. He moves carefully, gingerly, his body battered and bruised and sticky with blood, his head exploding with pain.

And then the wind intensifies and backs up to the north-east. It comes rampaging back with a long, deep moan. Then with a loud, thundering boom the roaring rumbling tidal wave surges in, spitting rocks, sucking sand, swamping the land. It rolls on endlessly, snapping trees, ripping boats from anchor chains, driving vessels over sand and miles inland.

Sea Devil crashes onto the rocks. She topples and plunges, a splintering crack in her hull. Wesley shrieks as she rolls and smashes and breaks apart. 'Voices call to me . . . my elders,' he cries, dragged down with the undertow.

The mountainous sea crashes over Sario, smashing him, pounding him. He tries to swim up to find air, to kick from its powerful force, but he's too weak, gulping in seawater – *drowning?*

Suddenly he's lifted on a massive wave, a fountain pushes him up. It carries him inland and gushes him out. Sario clings to wood, vomiting, bleeding, exhausted. He floats among matter, barely conscious, the rain pelting him like pebbles. But the storm is done, the waves subsiding. There's sand beneath him. He has to find shelter . . . sleep.

He peers through the murky grey daylight. The destruction is sickening: debris piled high around him, broken boats, broken bodies, birds and fish flapping and dying, trapped in nets and rigging. He can make out a wreck afloat in the distance, and movement close by – two arms struggling, a tangle of netting. Someone's alive!

Sario wades out, unsteady, stumbling through rubbish and broken cargo, through the seaweed and dying creatures washing in and out with the tide. The body is heavy and he struggles to lift it. He hauls the arms over a barrel and floats the limp form slowly to shore. He rolls the battered man over and feels for a pulse. 'Hiroshi?'

He drags Hiroshi up the beach through the pelting rain, looking for shelter, anything not buried under the sand. He sees an upturned dinghy jammed in the tree stumps, the trunks snapped. He rolls Hiroshi under the dinghy, and collapses exhausted on the wet ground beside him. Another body lies there injured and bleeding, face down. The boy moves.

'Wesley!'

'Come, brudda.' Wesley's long skinny arm reaches out and draws the boys close – all three battered and bleeding and clinging to a shaky lifeline.

Sario feels the warmth and closes his eyes. He won't starve or die of thirst with his mainland binghi friend. 'We be alright,' he whispers.

MARCH 5TH 1899

More than 300 people lost their lives when Hurricane Mahina slammed into the pearling fleet at Bathurst Bay.

Three days pass before Wesley's mob appear on the hill above the bay. They've travelled far to search for survivors and to salvage what they can from the wreckage. Wesley shouts and limps over the rubble, bruised and sore, but excited to see them. The men tend to the boys' cuts and bruises with their bush medicine. They rub sticks together and start a fire to cook them tucker.

Two sunrises later, when the boys have recovered enough to travel, Wesley waves down a rescue boat. 'Take boys to TI, cap'n,' he says, when the dinghy arrives. 'Them good divers.'

Hiroshi shakes his head. 'No more pearl-shell diving.' He's made new plans. 'I build fishing boats now.' Many luggers lie wrecked in the bay; he'll learn the trade and make good money. 'Pay back debt and help poor people in my village.' He smiles. 'I build you a long sleek island lugger, Sario.'

The captain says Thursday Island came through the storm and Sario thinks of Apu and Leilani. When Apu is better and they are back on their island, he will help his clan search for Thaati and Naku and Kadub. 'We buy island lugger, one day.'

The captain smiles. 'You will soon be able to buy a lugger of your own, boy,' he says. 'The Aboriginal Protection Fund will provide your clan with a fishing boat, and you can pay it off as you earn.'

Sario's eyes light with excitement. It's wonderful news. He'll work hard. Hiroshi can build the lugger and he'll skipper it! He turns to Wesley. 'You come? Join crew?'

Wesley shakes his head. 'Stay with my mob. Make spear. Go huntin'.' He won't leave his homeland ever again – except maybe to trade.

'We be alright,' Sario says, as he and Hiroshi climb into the canoe and wave goodbye. And they will.

Author's Note

Torres Strait is a spectacularly beautiful region, rich in culture and history. The Islanders are proud saltwater people, skilled in fishing, spear-hunting and seafaring. From the 1800s the harvesting of bêche de mer, trochus and pearl-shell brought economic benefits to Australia, but diver deaths and the exploitation of workers, including young children, proved a high price to pay. The often brutal history of this time is lesser-known, and a story I needed to tell.

The pearl-shell industry flourished within a decade of bêche-de-mer fishermen expanding into Torres Strait from the Pacific. The desperate need for workers was soon apparent. To fill the labour shortage, a large work-force known as Kanakas were imported from the Pacific Islands. They made a significant contribution to Australia's pearl-shell and sugar industries for more than forty years. An influx of Japanese, Malays, Chinese, Indians and others brought a multicultural mix to the islands, which continues today.

In 1901 at the time of Federation, a 'white population' was favoured. The migration and employment of non-white races was prohibited under the *Immigration Restriction Act* and *Pacific Island Labourers Act.* Despite regulation, some non-European and Asian divers continued to work in the Torres Strait, or were let in.

Many divers in the pearl-shell industry suffered and died from divers' disease, known as 'the bends'. This occurs when there is a rapid decrease in pressure, causing nitrogen bubbles to form in the blood upon ascent. A diver can suffer dizziness, shortness of breath and severe pain in the joints, with the body often staying in a bent position. 'Decompression', staging a diver's ascent to relieve symptoms, was not widely known or practised at the time of this story.

Due to the number of ships wrecked in the dangerous Torres Strait waters, the cave on the 'bird island' became an official refuge and ship's post office and operated for over a century. Captain James Cook named the island Booby Island in 1770 after the booby birds nesting there; its traditional name is Ngiangu. Remains of emergency stores were still in the cave as late as 1920. The lighthouse was manned for 102 years until the light was automated in 1992.

From 1903 island clans were able to purchase fishing boats using the pay-as-you-earn system. By 1906, seventeen island fishing boats were reported to be operating in Torres Strait waters. During the 1950s the pearl-shell industry declined due to the introduction of plastic to make buttons, and the depletion of pearl-oyster beds.

The distinctive white feathered headdress known as a *dhari* is worn in traditional ceremonies and dance. It features on the flag of the Torres Strait region along with a white five-pointed star symbolising the unity of the five major island groups. A broad panel of blue represents the sea, green bands at top and bottom the land, and thin black stripes the island people.

Acknowledgements

This is a work of fiction inspired by historical events of 1898 and 1899 in the Torres Strait. All characters are fictitious and do not relate to any island or clan in particular. Factual information comes from many sources and research has been thorough. Should there be any misinterpretation I sincerely apologise.

I acknowledge the Indigenous people of the Torres Strait Islands and Cape York Peninsula for passing on traditional legends and rich oral histories. I thank past researchers for compiling a wealth of information, including anthropologist A. C. Haddon, Captain John Foley, Regina Ganter, Gary Kerr, Ian Nicholson, memoir compiler Catherine Titasey. I also acknowledge Nola Ward Page of Thursday Island for her cultural advice and Mavis Bani of Torres Shire Council for her linguistic guidance and expertise, Debra Billson for the beautiful cover and text design, and the patient editorial team at Allen & Unwin, Eva Mills, Lyn White and Hilary Reynolds. I thank my husband Colin for his valuable input regarding boats, fishing and memories of his 'island boy' life in the Pacific.

The language used in this story is Mabuiag, recorded in the western islands of Torres Strait in the late 1880s by Cambridge anthropologists Sydney H. Ray and A. C. Haddon.

I acknowledge Ron Edwards for his updated language edition of 2001. Two traditional languages along with English form Torres Strait Creole, spoken in the islands today. Waiben (Thursday Island) is often spelled Waibene.

Timeline of the Torres Strait

In the last two decades, archaeologists have found evidence of human settlement in the Torres Strait dating back 2500 years.

1606 Luis Váez de Torres, a Spanish navigator, discovers the strait while sailing to Manila. Torres Strait carries his name.

1770 Captain James Cook anchors his ship HMB *Endeavour* at Possession Island and claims the east coast of Australia for Britain. He also names Booby Island (Ngiangu), where later a cave known as the Ocean Post Office is set up as a refuge and mail centre for European sea traffic.

1792 Kebisu, a Chief of Tudu Island, leads a canoe attack on the HMS *Providence*, commanded by Captain William Bligh, and the HMS *Assistant*, with midshipman Matthew Flinders on board. Several seamen are wounded. Bligh names the island Warrior Island.

1848 Captain Stanley, commander of HMS *Rattlesnake,* names three islands in the area: Wednesday, Thursday and Friday Islands.

1859 The colony of Queensland is formed.

1860s The Torres Strait becomes increasingly important as a trade route linking the Pacific and Indian Oceans. Shipwrecks increase. More navigational beacons are added and a shipping pilot service is suggested.

1864 A European settlement is established at Somerset on the eastern tip of Cape York. Commercial bêche-de-mer and trochus shell industries are established and South Sea Islander workers arrive from Asia and the Pacific.

1868 Captain Banner, a bêche-de-mer fisherman, visits Tudu (Warrior Island) and notices Islanders wearing pearl-shell ornaments. Commercial harvesting of pearl-shell begins in the Torres Strait.

1870s Shallow pearl-shell beds become depleted. Pump-boats are introduced, equipped with breathing helmets and rubberised canvas diving suits, allowing deep-sea diving. American and English clothing markets seek pearl-shell for buttons and buckles. The Torres Strait Islanders join the more than 500 Pacific Islanders (Kanakas) working on pearling boats. A period of extreme lawlessness, cruelty and treachery ensues as European lugger owners exploit Indigenous workers. The diver mortality rate is high.

1871 On 1 July, the London Missionary Society's (LMS) Reverend Samuel McFarlane arrives on Erub (Darnley Island). This event becomes known as the 'Coming of the Light' and is still celebrated annually throughout the Torres Strait. Christianity quickly becomes the dominant religion.

1873 British Parliament passes the *Imperial Pacific Islanders Protection Act,* known as the 'Kidnapping Act', to reduce 'blackbirding', a slavery practice prevalent from 1847–1904.

1877 Henry Marjoribanks Chester is appointed Police Magistrate and transfers the European settlement from Somerset to Waiben (Thursday Island), due to white-ant infestation, and strong sea currents making it difficult to moor ships.

1879 All the Torres Strait Islands are annexed and become Crown land. The *Queensland Coast Islands Act* grants control of the Islands, including the shell industries, to the Colony of Queensland. Islanders become British subjects.

1880s More than 100 luggers engage in the pearl-shell industry, with annual earnings over £25,000. European pearlers continue to exploit many of the Torres Strait Islander, Malay, Aboriginal and Filipino crewmen and divers. Diver fatalities continue to mar the industry.

1884 The *Native Labourers' Protection Act* is passed to regulate the employment of Indigenous Australians and Papua New Guineans on ships in Queensland waters.

1885 John Douglas is appointed government resident magistrate of Waiben (Thursday Island), which quickly becomes the headquarters of the pearling industry and a commercial centre. Islanders are not permitted to live on TI. More immigrants from Asia, the South Sea Islands and Europe arrive to work in the pearling industry. Japanese and Malays dominate the workforce.

1887 An underwater telegraph cable provides communication with mainland Australia, running between Waiben and Cape York.

1890s Torres Strait supplies over half the world's demand for pearl-shell. Further influx of indentured Japanese divers threatens employment of Torres Strait Islander divers. The discovery of the pearl-shell rich Darnley Deeps increases diver mortality. Disease and ransacking of islands reduces the Islander population.

1891 Green Hill Fort is constructed on TI to deter a Russian invasion. Floating stations or motherships are introduced to supply provisions to small luggers, allowing them to stay longer on shell-beds.

1897 Queensland Government passes the *Aboriginal Protection and Restriction of the Sale of Opium Act*, purportedly to protect Aboriginal peoples from the impact of white colonisation and introduced diseases. Their rights are severely affected, with consequences that include their removal to mission reserves and government guardianship over their children.

1899 Cyclone Mahina destroys a pearling fleet in Bathurst Bay, Cape York with more than 300 lives lost. It remains Australia's deadliest storm.

1901 The colony of Queensland becomes a state of the new Commonwealth of Australia. The *Immigration Restriction Act* of 1901, the 'White Australia Policy', is passed but Japanese are exempt due to their heavy involvement in the pearling trade. However, the *Pacific Islander Labourers Act* of 1901 orders the deportation of all South Sea Islanders to their home islands by 1906. This has significant repercussions for the pearling industry.

1904 Pacific Industry Limited is set up, enabling Torres Strait Islanders to operate their own boats. Almost 4000 pearling boats employ 2500 men at the peak of the pearling industry.

1920 All the major pearling companies are established on TI. New shell grounds buoy pearl-shell prices until the world is struck by the Great Depression of the 1930s.

1940s Post-war demand for pearl-shell and trochus is short-lived due to the discovery of plastic buttons and buckles and the eventual depletion of pearl-shell beds.

1960s Pearl-culture farms, mainly run by Japanese entrepreneurs, become the new focus for the pearling industry in the Torres Strait.

Mabuiag Glossary

aka-pali frightened
apu mother
babat brother/sister
baidam shark
burum pig
butu sand
buuzi vine
dawa banana
dhangal dugong
dhari headdress of white feathers
eso thanks
gabun-mai heal
gasamai catch
getalai crab
gorsar plenty
guul canoe
iawai journey
idi oil
kai kai food (Torres Strait Creole)
kaiwa island
kapu beautiful
kemu plant
kikiri sick pain
kuik head
kumala sweet potato (Torres Strait Creole)
kursi hammerhead shark
launga no
lukup medicine
maalu sea
mabaeg/mabaegal man/men
malil metal
markai European, spirit being
mital sweet
mui fire
ngoka girl
nutai try, tempt
paekau butterfly
pagami sew
sapur fruit bat, flying fox
sop sop traditional food (Torres Strait Creole)
thaati father
tik bait

tu smoke
upiri poison
uzari go
wakain-tamai think
waku mat
wapi fish
waru turtle
warup drum

About the Author

Kay began her writing career with feature articles for newspapers and lifestyle magazines before moving into writing educational material for children. Her interest in history was fostered when commissioned to write *Patch Parker: Son of a Convict*, now a recommended resource by the History Teachers' Association. Research into lesser-known history took her to Torres Strait and the tumultuous time of Federation. Kay's work in schools with reluctant readers spanned twenty-six years and prompts her to write history simply. Other of her works feature animals and the environment, including the non-fiction book *Introduced Species in Australia*, commended in the Whitley Awards by the Royal Zoological Society of New South Wales.

Kay grew up in Sydney and moved with her husband and children to remote areas of Tasmania and Western Australia before settling in Far North Queensland, where two spectacular environments meet: the Daintree Rainforest and the Great Barrier Reef.